The
Muddle-headed
Wombat

The Adventures of
The
Muddle-headed
Wombat

story by
RUTH PARK

illustrated by
Noela Young

🏛 Angus&Robertson
An imprint of HarperCollins*Publishers*

Angus&Robertson
An imprint of HarperCollins*Publishers,* Australia

The Muddle-headed Wombat first published in 1962
The Muddle-headed Wombat at School first published in 1962
The Muddle-headed Wombat on Holiday first published in 1964
The Muddle-headed Wombat in the Treetops first published in 1965
Combined edition first published in Australia by Angus & Robertson Publishers in 1979
First published in Australia by Angus & Robertson Publishers in 1939
Reprinted in 1980, 1981, 1983, 1985, 1989, 1990
Commemorative edition 1986, reprinted in 1989
Classics edition 1990, reprinted 1991, 1995, 1996, 1998, 1999, 2000, 2001 (twice), 2002
by HarperCollins*Publishers* Pty Limited
ABN 36 009 913 517
A member of the HarperCollins*Publishers* (Australia) Pty Limited Group
www.harpercollins.com.au

Copyright individual editions © Kemalde Pty Ltd 1962, 1964, 1965
Copyright combined edition © Kemalde Pty Ltd 1979

HarperCollins*Publishers*
25 Ryde Road, Pymble, Sydney, NSW 2073, Australia
31 View Road, Glenfield, Auckland 10, New Zealand
77-85 Fulham Palace Road, London W6 8JB, United Kingdom
Hazelton Lanes, 55 Avenue Road, Suite 2900, Toronto, Ontario M5R 3L2
and 1995 Markham Road, Scarborough, Ontario M1B 5M8, Canada
10 East 53rd Street, New York NY 10022, USA

National Library of Australia Cataloguing-in-Publication data:

Park, Ruth.
The adventures of the muddle-headed wombat.
ISBN 0 207 16733 8.
1. Wombats – Juvenile fiction.
I. Title. (Series : Australian children's classics (Angus&Robertson)).
A823.2.

Printed and bound in Australia by Griffin Press on 80gsm Econoprint

15 14 13 12   02 03 04 05

Contents

The Muddle-headed Wombat

CHAPTER I

Let's Meet Wombat

THERE was once a muddle-headed wombat sitting in the grass and feeling very lonely.

A wombat is a square animal with thick hair like a door-mat, stumpy legs, and no tail to speak of. He has brown eyes and a comfortable, leathery flat nose like a koala.

This wombat was lonely because he had no sisters or brothers or aunties or uncles, and besides, he had spent all his pocket money.

"I wish I had a friend," he thought, "a nice, comfy little friend who would fit in my cardigan pocket. A wombat could have lots of adventures with a friend like that."

Suddenly, in the paddock nearby, he saw a wooden man waving his wooden arms and squeaking a song of his own, squeak-creak, squeak-squawk! He was a scarecrow. He wore a raggy old coat and a big straw hat, and yellow gloves on his wooden hands. Wombat was pleased to see him.

"Perhaps I could make friends with him! Yoo-hoo, Mr Scarecrow, here comes your little wombat!"

Every time the wind puffed over the gullies, the wooden man swung his arms to left and right. Wombat thought the scarecrow was waving to him. He stood up on his hind legs and pulled at the scarecrow's coat.

"Here I am! Are you pleased I'm here?"

Thump! Down came the scarecrow's wooden hand on Wombat's head. Wombat was very cross. He didn't understand that it was the wind's fault.

"That's a horribubble thing to do to a new friend," he growled. "You're a hidjus old pollywobble! I'm going to push you over, that's what I'm going to do!"

And he put his forehead against the post which held the scarecrow in its place, and he pushed and pushed until there was a creak and a crack and down went the wooden man all in a heap. Away bowled his straw hat, with Wombat trundling after it. It was such a friendly-looking hat, with a raggy brim, and a great many windows in the crown, that Wombat put it on.

"Anyway, you and I can be friends, you dear old hat!" he said.

All at once Wombat heard a queer little noise. It was like a fairy sobbing. Wombat *was* excited.

"Do you hear that, you dear old hat? That's a very little animal being sad and miserabubble."

He hurried over to the edge of the road, and peered in amongst the tall grass stalks. There he saw the tiniest, furriest animal, rolled into a ball and crying to itself. Wombat had a soft heart. He couldn't bear this sad sight. A tear ran down his nose and plopped on the stranger's little head. At once it unrolled itself, sat up, and said angrily: "And now it's raining! Oh, this is an awful day for me!"

Wombat liked the little animal's pink, piggy nose and soft grey fur. He liked the way it carried its long tail over its arm as though it were the train on an evening dress. He chuckled.

"It isn't raining at all. It's me . . . crying."

"Well, don't cry on me, whoever you are. I have enough troubles already."

As it spoke, the little animal closed up its mouth in a tight, worried way, and began pawing around in the grass.

"I'm looking for my glasses," it explained. "I've dropped them somewhere and I can't find them. Oh, bother, bother, bother!"

6

Wombat was happy to help look for the glasses. He was very good at losing things, so he thought that perhaps he'd be good at finding them, too. He scrabbled about in the grass roots, and in a moment he had found the lost spectacles. They were just about as tiny as spectacles can get. In fact, the little animal used a sweetpea pod for carrying them around. Wombat was happy he had been so useful.

"Aren't I a smart wombat, eh? Aren't I?" he kept saying.

"I'll see in a moment," said the little animal. It put on the glasses and looked at Wombat. It started at his toes and worked upwards, and by the time it had reached the top of his head it had a crick in its neck.

"You really are dreadfully big," it complained.

"I can fold up a bit. You watch," said Wombat eagerly, and he pulled in his toes, and humped down his neck, and flattened out his ears. "I'm really terribubbly small, you know."

The little animal took no notice. "You don't look very sensible, either."

"I've got lots of brains," said Wombat. "You listen to them rattle."

He shook his head and it rattled beautifully.

"My!" said the little animal.

Wombat was very interested in his new friend. "I can see you're a mouse. Are you like the mouses that live in houses?"

"Certainly not!" The Mouse's nose turned as red as a radish with indignation. "I'm a fat-tailed, pouched Bush Mouse, and don't you forget it."

Wombat didn't have to ask the Mouse to come and live with him and share his adventures. The Mouse liked Wombat. It liked his stumpy paws and his muddled-up whiskers. It decided it might as well live in his big straw hat as anywhere else.

The Mouse scooted up Wombat's arm and under his hat. The next moment its long, pink nose stuck out through the hole in the front.

"Oh, what a lovely view there is from up here, Wombat!"

"That's all very well, Mouse, but it's not my hat, you know. I have to give it back to the old wooden man I pushed over."

Wombat trundled back to the paddock to see whether the old wooden man had got up again. There he was, the silly old fellow, still lying on the ground.

"Come on, up you get, don't sulk!"

He tugged at the scarecrow's yellow glove, and all at once the wooden man came to pieces. His straw stuffing fell out. His sugar-bag waistcoat came off and his wooden arms clattered to the ground. There was nothing left but his goggly painted face on the end of a broomstick. Wombat's eyes almost popped out.

8

"Oh, Mouse, look what your wombat has done! I've killed him dead as dead can be."

"Now, now, you can't do that to a wooden man," answered the Mouse, calmly polishing its glasses with the end of its tail. "And besides, the farmer is coming, so you'll be able to explain."

The farmer wasn't cross. He said the old scarecrow needed to be pulled down, anyway. He didn't mind if Wombat took away the old straw hat. Wombat was happy and Mouse was happy. Mouse was so happy that it decided to give Wombat a little present.

"I hope it's a banana," said Wombat.

"No, it's this," said Mouse, and it took out of its pouch something very small and silvery. Wombat put it up close to his eyes, then he held it away as far as he could. Still he couldn't make out what it was.

"Silly," said little Mouse. "It's for music. It's a mouth organ."

Wombat lay down on his back and kicked his short legs in the air for joy. He had never seen anything quite as cute as this tiny, tiny mouth organ. The Mouse played a bar or two of music. It was as high and thin as the music that crickets make. Then Mouse said it would teach Wombat to play, if he'd stand up and stop kicking.

"Take a deep breath, Wombat, and make a good big noise!"

So he did. He took a deep breath, and he blew, and the mouth organ gave a beautiful squawk. Then he drew in his breath again, and this time the mouth organ went with it. It vanished altogether inside his mouth. He heard it give a sad little squeak as it arrived somewhere inside him, under the last button of his cardigan.

Mouse was furious. "It wasn't very good-mannered of you to swallow my present, Wombat!"

Wombat hadn't meant to swallow it. What good was it down there? He felt very sad. Then he noticed that every time he breathed, the mouth organ made a musical sound.

"Do you know what, Mouse? Soon I'll be able to play a tune on my breath."

The Mouse glared at him.

"But don't you see, Mouse? If I can play a tune on my breath and sing a song, then people might give us pennies. And, Mouse, we could save up and buy a bike."

"With red wheels?" asked the Mouse, who liked to get everything straight.

So it was agreed. They found a little town, and a street, and a corner, and there they stood, blushing, and twiddling their paws, and trying not to mind when people stared at them. The Mouse held Wombat's ankle tightly. It was nervous lest one of those big shoes passing by should tread on it.

Wombat knew a tune. It was "My Bonnie Lies Over the Ocean." It sounded like this:

"My bony lies over the ocean, my bony lies over the sea.
 Oh, please won't you hear my commotion, and give lots
   of pennies to me?"

Then he took off his hat and trundled around amongst the crowd. He got four pennies and five threepences, and one creamy toffee, which he liked even more than the threepences. He and Mouse were very happy. They thought they would be able to save up for their bike very quickly. Then along came a Policeman.

"Now then, now then," he said to Wombat. "In this town people are not allowed to play musical instruments in the street for money."

"But he wasn't," said Mouse, popping its head out of Wombat's sleeve.

"I just play on my breath," said Wombat proudly, and he gave a wonderfully musical cough for the Policeman.

The Policeman walked right around Wombat. He looked him over carefully. There was no mouth organ to be seen. Perhaps Wombat was telling the truth. But still the Policeman had his duty to do.

"You'd better come along with me and see the Sergeant," he said.

Wombat was excited. He had never seen a Sergeant. He jumped up and down with joy, and poor Mouse fell out of his sleeve. It scrambled back into his hat just in time before the Policeman trod on it by mistake.

They were taken along to the Sergeant's desk at the police station. The Mouse sat on the ink-bottle and explained what happened. The Sergeant said that Wombat couldn't be blamed for playing music in the street when all he had done was to breathe.

Meanwhile, Mouse was looking about the police station. Huddled up on a chair in one corner was a grey tabby cat. He was skinny and miserable and he had a peaky little face with big ears. He wore a bright red bow tie, but anyone could see it hadn't been washed and ironed for weeks.

"Oh, my," thought tender-hearted Mouse. "That cat is a stray cat. Anyone can see he has no one to love him."

Mouse began to wonder if, by any chance, a mouse could keep a pet cat of its own?

CHAPTER II

Here Comes Tabby

MOUSE tweaked at the Sergeant's shoe-laces.

"If no one else wants that cat," it said, "may I have him?"

The Sergeant was pleased. He did not really want a police station cat because he had one already. But Wombat felt very jealous and bristly. He made a grumble-umble sound deep in his middle.

"Why do you want a cat when you've got me, Mouse, eh?" he asked.

"Because he's such a skinny, squeaky, plain little cat," explained Mouse. "Poor thing."

Wombat made the grumble-umble noise again, and this time it got mixed up with the mouth organ and with one last horrid drone the mouth organ became silent.

"See what you've made me do?" scolded Wombat. "Now I can't play on my breath, and how will we get pennies to buy a bike with red wheels?"

But Mouse wasn't listening. It had scampered over to the cat and was bouncing up and down and twinkling its spectacles.

"Would you like to come and live with Wombat and me and be our second-best friend and have adventures, and save up for a bike with red wheels?"

The cat nodded.

"What's your name?" asked Mouse.

"Vernon la Puss," said the cat in a low trembling voice.

"Oh, it is not," said Wombat, "you're making up stories. I can tell by your droopy whiskers. Haven't you a sensibubble name like Mouse or Wombat?"

The cat wiped away a tear. "I just made it up because it sounds so grand. My name's really just Tabby Cat, and nobody loves me."

"Come on, then," said Mouse, "and Wombat and I will love you."

Wombat wasn't a bit sure that he wanted to love Tabby Cat. He knew he didn't want his nice little Mouse to love Tabby Cat. He felt very jealous. He wasn't even very pleased when the kind police sergeant gave him a water-pistol he'd found a long time before. He trundled along the road behind Tabby Cat and Mouse, and grumble-umbled to himself.

Mouse knew stray cats are usually hungry. Mouse bought some fish for Tabby, who had brightened up a lot since he had found some friends. Mouse also bought some orange drink for Wombat.

"Now, let's be happy!"

"I'm happy," said Tabby. "Fish is my favourite fruit!"

Suddenly Wombat felt so jealous he couldn't bear it any more. He dipped the water-pistol into his orange juice, filled it up, and shot Tabby in the waistcoat.

It was quite the most terrible thing he had ever done. Mouse didn't squeak to him for hours. As for Tabby, he licked and picked and picked and licked and still he felt sticky and orange-y.

Wombat was ashamed of himself.

"I'm very sorry, Tabby," he said. "Would you like me to wash you with soap and water and peg you out by the ears to dry?"

Tabby gave a miaow of terror. He darted up a tree and sat there crying.

"Nobody loves me. I told you. People *always* shoo me away and stand on my tail and shoot me with orange drink. Oh, I wish I weren't me!"

The Mouse tapped its pink foot in a fierce way. "I'm ashamed of you, Wombat. Now, what can we do to help Tabby?"

Then it had an idea.

"What about a vacuum cleaner?"

"What's a what'sname, Mouse, eh?" asked Wombat hopefully.

"It's a sort of machine that sucks the dust out of carpets. If we used one on Tabby Cat, we could get every scrap of orange off his fur."

"Let's try it on Wombat first," said Tabby. "I'm a delicate pussy."

Wombat didn't mind. Wombat very much wanted to help. They went to a shop that sold carpets and explained to the man what they wanted to do. He was very helpful. He turned on the carpet cleaner and Tabby began to run the nozzle up and down Wombat's thick, tously, brown hair. It tickled Wombat very much. He rolled on the floor giggling. Mouse was delighted.

"You look so handsome, Wombat! Oh, I wish I weren't a small animal! Then I could be vacuumed, too."

Then it was Tabby's turn.

"You be careful, Wombat. I don't want my ears turned inside-out or my whiskers knotted."

Wombat turned on the cleaner. He went up and down, up and down Tabby's back.

"There are lots of grey spots here and I want to get them off."

"You silly old muddle-head," cried Tabby, "those spots grow on me! After all, I *am* a tabby cat."

"Don't you tell me I've got a head like a muddle," growled Wombat. "*You've* got a head like a bicycle seat."

Just then the nozzle fell off the vacuum cleaner, and poor Tabby flew straight up the pipe.

There was a gurgly sound in the pipe, and then the cleaner went on buzzing as though nothing had happened. Wombat turned the cleaner off, and he and Mouse peered down the pipe.

"Oh, Wombat, you are awful!" said Mouse, but it couldn't help giggling.

"Is it nice in there, Tabby?" called Wombat. "I wish I could get in there and listen to the motor humming."

But Tabby didn't answer. Mouse and Wombat sat down and looked at the cleaner for a while, then they thought that perhaps they'd better unscrew it and see how Tabby was getting along. Luckily the first thing Wombat unscrewed was the bit at the end where you take out the dust. Out came all kinds of interesting things; little balls of cotton, scraps of straw, pins and tacks, and a great, furry, grey wad of dust.

"Oooh, Tabby," whispered Mouse, "that isn't *you?*"

The furry ball of dust gave a great sneeze.

"We found him," beamed Wombat, "aren't we terribubbly smart?"

Some of the dust fell off and there was Tabby, wearing a woolly grey overcoat of dust, and a little beret of fluff on his head. Two yellow eyes glared out of the dust. Wombat was very surprised.

"However did you get so dirty, Tabby? I thought the middle of a cleaner would be as clean as clean."

Tabby sneezed. "I shall never forgive you, Wombat!" he said.

"But Tabby, I didn't put you inside the cleaner. I just pointed it at you and in you flew, like a bird, Tab."

Tabby twitched his ears and out fluttered some pieces of red and blue wool that had come out of the carpet.

"I'm not going to be friends with you, Wombat. Not if you go down on bended paws."

Wombat took off his hat and began to cry into it.

"Perhaps I *have* a head like a muddle. I *am* sorry, Tabby. Don't be cross, Tabby."

"He didn't mean to be unkind," pleaded Mouse.

Tabby twitched his whiskers haughtily. The dust flew out in clouds.

"A cat has his pride," he said. "Good-bye forever."

Mouse was small, but it was smart. It knew Tabby really didn't want to go away. So it said sadly:

"What a pity! I thought you could have your photograph taken when we have ours done. I *would* like a photograph of you, Tabby dear."

Wombat stopped crying. He was about to say, "What photograph?" but Mouse bit him on the toe just in time to stop him. Mouse had a feeling that Tabby Cat was very conceited, so it said even more sadly:

"Well, good-bye, Tabby dear. Don't let us stop you."

"We-ell," said Tabby, "I wouldn't mind having a picture of myself to send to my Uncle Tom."

Wombat was delighted. "You lucky, lucky puss to have a nuncle, I haven't anyone. Is he a cat like you?"

"Silly," said Tabby. He curled up his whiskers. "I just *might* get my picture taken, Mouse, to please you."

Mouse knew they had just enough money to pay a photographer. The bike with red wheels would have to wait.

The photographer was pleased to see them. He arranged Tabby looking at a flower.

"Just pretend it's a sardine," said Wombat, "and you'll look lovely."

Tabby showed all his sharp teeth in a very sweet smile, the camera clicked, and it was all over.

"Oh, how happy Uncle Tom will be when he gets a picture of handsome me!" said Tabby as he jumped down from the chair. Now it was Mouse's turn. Mouse arranged its ears and its whiskers, draped its tail gracefully over one arm, smiled when it was told, and was photographed.

"What a very intelligent small animal!" said the photographer.

Now it was Wombat's turn. He would not take off his old straw hat.

"But you must," said Tabby. "Otherwise you'll look just like a haystack."

Wombat stuck out his lip. "My hat want its picture taken, too."

"Please, Wombat," said Mouse, stroking his ankle lovingly. So Wombat took off his hat, told it he wouldn't be long, and sat before the camera. He didn't like it at all. His back legs kept slipping from the chair, and his nose began to itch.

"Wombat, leave that nose alone!" ordered Tabby.

"It's my nose, you old cat," said Wombat crossly.

"Please try and sit still," said the photographer.

"Treely ruly I'm trying," said Wombat. "For you, Mouse," he said.

At last all was ready. The photographer was hidden beneath his black cloth. Wombat was grumble-umbling to himself. Mouse was waggling its ears so that Wombat would smile.

"No, no, there's some mud on his nose!" cried Tabby, and he dashed forward to brush it off just as the camera clicked.

"You wicked cat, you've spoiled the picture!" said the photographer. He was so upset that he wouldn't come out from under his black cloth. But Mouse sat on his shoe and argued. Mouse coaxed him to develop the picture so that they could have a look at it.

"Yes, I shall," said the photographer, "if you promise to go away and never come back. I'm not strong enough for wombats, really I'm not!"

The picture was a great surprise. It wasn't like Tabby, it wasn't like Wombat. There was Wombat's tubby form sitting on the chair. There was Tabby's catty little face on top of it. Yet somehow the Tabby face had short, stubby Wombat ears, and somehow the stout shape of Wombat had a long, grey catty tail.

"I shall never live down the shame!" said Tabby.

But Mouse entered the photograph in a funny pictures competition, and it won! It was called "The Wonderful Womcat," and won five pounds!

Tabby couldn't believe it.

Wombat couldn't believe it.

"It won't be long before we have our bike with red wheels!" said sensible Mouse.

CHAPTER III

Everyone Loves the Circus

ONE morning Wombat woke up, and straightaway he felt so happy he had to stand on his head. Luckily it had a nice flat top, so he was able to balance, waving his legs and making happy sounds.

Tabby was very cross. "Nobody cares whether a cat gets any sleep around here!" he complained. But Wombat fell on his back and kicked his legs and sang:

"Something excitabubble is going to happen today!"

"How do you know, Wombat?" asked Mouse, very interested.

"I feel it in my bones," said Wombat. He looked under his cardigan and pointed to a rib on the left side. "*That* bone."

"I don't believe your bones," said Tabby scornfully. But just then all three animals heard a wonderful sound. It was a band. They rushed to the side of the road. What did they see? They saw a procession of red and yellow wagons drawn by black and white spotty horses.

"Wheeeeee!" cried Mouse. "A circus!"

In front rode a clown with a green suit with moons and stars all over it. At the back could be seen two elephants, each wearing a kind of crown of red silk fringed with gold. Oh, how exciting!

"Told you," said Wombat.

"Perhaps if we fed the horses and washed the elephants they'd let us in to see the show for free!" cried Tabby Cat.

Wombat liked that idea. He put Mouse in his hat, carefully tucking in all stray ends of tail. Then he took Tabby by the paw and they hurried along and joined on the end of the circus procession.

The first wagon had stopped beside a big paddock at the roadside, and already men were busily carrying out poles, ropes, and a billowy mountain of tent.

Wombat trundled forward at such a rate he hauled Tabby off his feet. He sailed through the air behind Wombat, his tail streaming out like a flag, and they all arrived at the very spot where the men were putting up the tent.

"Please, please give us a job," gasped Tabby.

"That all depends," said the Head Man. "How much wages do you want?"

"We don't want wages," said Mouse. "We just like working for the circus!"

So the Head Man gave them all jobs. How their hearts thumped! Their paws felt cold and trembly and Mouse's glasses misted with excitement. A job in a circus!

"I'm going to be a lion tamer!" said Mouse.

"I shall do wonderful tricks on the swings, and everyone will say, 'Oh, just look at that handsome puss!'" boasted Tabby.

"I just want to pat the ellafumps on their lovely long noses," said Wombat.

But it happened differently.

Mouse was put in charge of a trained beetle act. It had to perch on a table in one of the sideshows outside the big tent, and take care of all the educated beetles. Mouse was insulted.

"Who wants to look after a silly old beetle?"

"But these are trained beetles, Mouse. They're very clever. Look, Wombat!" said Tabby. They peered into the glass-topped box where six big black beetles pulled tiny golden coaches, or combed their whiskers in front of looking-glasses as big as shillings.

"Oh, pooh!" said Mouse. But as they went away Wombat and Tabby could hear Mouse piping: "Roll up and see the Brilliant Black Beetles! Beautiful black beetles that have performed before all the crowned heads of Europe. Roll up! Roll up!"

"If Mouse is terribubbly good with the beetles, the Head Man might allow it to tame lions later on," said Wombat.

Wombat and Tabby had to sweep out the ring and make themselves useful. They wore old shabby uniforms, not at all like the red and gold ones they had dreamed about. They swept their very best, because, like Mouse, they hoped to get a better job later on.

Wombat dreamed a bit while he was sweeping.

"I might get a job riding an ellafump. Or perhaps one of the lions will put its dear old head into my mouth and everyone will cheer!"

He was so busy dreaming he did not notice he had swept himself right out of the big tent and into another, a little tent with boxes and cages all around it. Wombat poked into them all, but they were all empty. At last he came to a cage that was glassed-in all round.

Wombat thought he might climb inside and have a quiet sleep.

So he had a little sleep, and when he awakened he discovered a very strange thing. A large green snake had curled itself cosily around his middle. A yellow snake was looking out of his cardigan pocket.

"I expect I'm still dreaming," said Wombat. He closed his eyes and counted up to four frontwards and then backwards, which was as far as he could go. Then he opened his eyes.

"Bother! Still here."

Then he noticed that another snake was curled around the crown of his dear old hat, just like a ribbon. Wombat became very angry, for his hat was his greatest treasure.

"Get off my hat, you big *worm*!"

He heard Tabby calling outside the cage. Tabby opened the door and peered in.

"Have you seen Mouse, Wombat? I can't find it anywhere!"

"You've lost my mouse!" Wombat was very upset. "I've got to go and look for it. Here, hold these snakes for me!"

Wombat tore the snakes off himself and draped them over Tabby.

"You look after those snakes, Tab. They aren't ours, you know, so be careful."

Wombat hurried out of the cage and rushed off to look for Mouse. Tabby just stood. His tail went to sleep and there were

pins and needles in every paw. He dared not flicker a whisker.

Wombat did not come back, but after a while there was a merry whistle and in came the Keeper. He *was* surprised to see Tabby. He went into the cage and unwound the snakes. Tabby didn't say, "Thank you." He just went on standing there, his tail drooping and his ears flattened.

"Poor old cat, you've had a shock," said the Keeper. "Didn't you know those snakes are harmless? Well, the best thing for a shocked cat is a nice bit of fish."

He patted Tabby on the head. Tabby fell forward as stiff as a post, and the Keeper caught him.

"Ah, you'll be all right after a good meal of fish, my boy," he said and he carried Tabby over to the big ice-box which stood near the seals' tank. On the way he met Wombat, still running around looking for Mouse and making loud sorrowful sounds.

"No, I'm *not* going to look for your Mouse," said the Keeper. "I've got this shocked cat to look after."

"Tabby, Tabby, wake up! Oooh, whatever will I do without my very own second-best friend?" cried Wombat.

"You can give him a piece of fish out of the ice-box. I've other things to do."

Wombat didn't like seeing Tabby as stiff as a post. He was worried about Tabby, but he was more worried about Mouse because Mouse was such a very small animal.

"Suppose a lion ate it? Oh, what a horribubble thought!"

And in his worry Wombat quite forgot what he was supposed to do and popped Tabby inside the ice-box and went off, forgetting all about him.

Tabby had not been inside the ice-box five seconds before his whiskers wiggled and his tail began to lash hungrily.

"Oh, look, look . . . cod . . . snapper . . . salmon . . . and dear little squidgy sardines! What shall I eat first?"

Though Tabby was a well-mannered cat, he ate and ate until he could hardly move.

"Just one more sardine and I'll go."

But he had no room for the sardine. He had to put it in his pocket and stagger out of the ice-box. He tottered around the circus until he came to the little room where the bandsmen kept their instruments. There he met Wombat, who was crying into his hat.

"Can't find Mouse anywhere, Tabby."

"Ur," said Tabby.

Wombat looked at him. He was a pale green cat instead of a grey one.

"What's the matter with *you*, you ole cat?"

"Ur," said Tabby.

Wombat frowned at Tabby.

"That's not a nice thing to say to a poor Wombat with a losted Mouse, Tabby."

"I feel as though my head is on the wrong way around," moaned poor Tabby.

"Well, perhaps it is," said Wombat kindly. Then he shook his head. "No, because your tail and your face are still on different sides."

The Head Man came stamping along. "Where's that Mouse and where are my beetles?" he shouted.

Tabby and Wombat couldn't imagine why the beetles had gone too, unless they had kidnapped Mouse.

"I'm not a bit satisfied with any of you," shouted the Head Man, who felt very upset about his beetles. "Just wait till I catch that Mouse!"

"Someone calling me?" said a little voice, and out of a curly big golden musical instrument crawled Mouse, looking very spruce and carrying a brown paper parcel.

"Where are my *beetles*?" yelled the Head Man.

"Safely in this parcel," explained Mouse. "I really got very tired of looking after them, so I thought we'd all have a little sleep, and we *do* feel better; isn't that nice?"

The beetles looked quite happy, though perhaps their legs were a little tangled. But the Head Man wasn't pleased.

"Look at this Wombat! He didn't sweep the tent at all well. Look at that pale sick cat . . . good for nothing."

"Ur!" said Tabby.

"And now Mouse goes off with my beetles. What you three need is a hard job. I'm going to put you into the lion taming business. That will smarten you up."

The Head Man thought Wombat and Tabby and Mouse would be scared. But they weren't.

CHAPTER IV

The Lion Tamer

ALTHOUGH they had just received the exciting news that they were going to work as lion tamers, Tabby still looked very pale and droopy.

Mouse jumped into Tabby's pocket to comfort him. The next moment Mouse bounced out again.

"Eeeeeek, there's an awful dead fish in here, Tabby!"

"Yes, I know," said Tabby in a pale way, "but I don't want it. *You* have it, Wombat."

Wombat didn't like fish. But he didn't want to hurt Tabby's feelings, so he took the sardine and put it inside his hat. Then they went off to the Lion's cage.

Wombat beamed at the lion. "She's a lady lion, and she is old and kind-hearted, and she never bites anyone!"

"Do you think," said Mouse nervously, "that perhaps . . . perhaps I'm a teeny bit small to be a lion tamer?"

"Of course you aren't, Mouse," said Wombat. "But I'll go in the cage first just to show you what a terribubbly kind old lady she is."

Wombat undid the cage and climbed in. Tabby quickly did the lock up again. He felt he wasn't quite strong enough for lions just yet, especially after all the fish he'd eaten.

"I'm a very delicate pussy, you know," he muttered to himself.

Wombat trundled up to the Lioness. He liked her big, paddy, yellow paws. And the Lioness liked him. She reached out and gave him a tremendous lick which would have taken his nose off if it hadn't been fiat already.

"And I love you, too!" said Wombat.

The Lioness made a rumbly sound like a giant purr. She picked Wombat up by the scruff of the neck and carried him into the middle of the cage. She lay down with him before her fore paws and began to lick him, like a mother cat.

"I had a wash yesterday! Tell her, Mouse," protested Wombat. But Mouse was trembling like a leaf.

"Now, that's enough," said Wombat. "You've got to learn some tricks, that's what I'm here for. No more face washes. After all, I'm a lion tamer."

"Clever little cubby wubby," said the Lioness, kissing Wombat on one ear and almost blowing it off.

"Don't call names," said Wombat. The Lioness kissed the other ear.

Wombat shook his head. He wished Mouse or Tabby would advise him on what a wombat did when he was mistaken for a lion's child.

Then he thought: "If I say I'm not her cub, she might whack me with one of those terribubbly big paws and then I'd get dented. I'd better pretend."

"Mummy!" he cried.

"Cubby!" said the Lioness.

He trundled into her paws and nestled against her side, which smelt a bit like old bones and hay. It made Wombat sneeze, though it was really the sort of perfume he liked.

Mouse darted between the bars of the cage like a pink bat and bit the Lioness on the nose.

"You leave my Wombat alone!" squeaked Mouse, its glasses glittering with rage. "Come and help, Tabby!"

And Tabby did. He was shaking with fear, for he really was a timid cat, but he unlocked the cage and went inside.

"I've got something for you, Mrs Lion," said Tabby in a trembly voice. And he took Wombat's hat from his head. He had remembered that little squidgy unwanted sardine. There it was, sitting on top of Wombat's head, a little squashed and second hand, but still fish. And Tabby knew all cats like fish. With a beautiful bow he handed it to the Lioness. Mouse scuttled like a flash up Wombat's leg and hid under his cardigan. Wombat trundled out of the cage.

"Fish!" said the Lioness. "My favourite fruit!"

When she had finished the fish she said to Tabby:

"Are *you* my own little cubby?"

"I'll try," said Tabby. The Lioness whispered: "You know, a moment ago there was a fat brown animal in here, and he pretended to be my cub. But you look *much* more like my cubby."

"That's because I'm a handsome cat," said Tabby. "But I'll only be your cub if you do all the tricks I'm supposed to teach you. Will you?"

The Lioness promised. She liked Tabby much more than Wombat because he was like a little tabby lion.

So Tabby became the lion tamer. He wore a splendid uniform of red, with many gold buttons. The Lioness did everything he told her to do, and Tabby was clapped more loudly than anyone. No one knew that the Lioness was obeying him just because she loved him.

Tabby became even more conceited. Wombat thought that if he were sat on once or twice, and flattened out like a bookmark, it would do him the world of good.

Perhaps Wombat was grumble-umbling because he was a
little bit jealous. He and Mouse had been set to watch over
Charlie, the big grey monkey. Mouse had to brush Charlie's
clothes and shine his buttons, and see that his vegetable mash
was nice and hot. Wombat had to lead him into the ring and
put him through his tricks. But of course Charlie's tricks did
not bring as much clapping as the old Lioness's tricks. Also
Wombat's uniform was not as grand as Tabby's beautiful red
and golden one.

Wombat poked out his tongue at Charlie, and Charlie
poked out his. Charlie didn't like having his keeper make
faces at him, and in his clever monkey mind he resolved to
get his own back.

Wombat watched the way Tabby bowed to every corner of the big tent when he had finished his act. Wombat thought maybe he could do that, too. He bowed all around, and Mouse, who was inside his hat getting a good view of everything, almost fell out one of the holes. Chattering shrilly, Charlie jumped on Wombat's back, wound long, grey, hairy arms around his neck and pulled him down into the sawdust with a thump.

The people at the circus thought this was all part of the act. They laughed and clapped. Wombat tried to get up, but Charlie sat on him and poured sawdust into his ears.

"You stop that, you ole pollywobble!" growled Wombat.

Mouse darted out of the hat to scold Charlie, and had a little pile of sawdust at once heaped on its head. Mouse darted back into the hat very quickly.

"Let me up, you hidjus old Charlie!" roared Wombat.

Then Charlie thought he had better do something really clever. He undid Wombat's uniform coat and took it off. He put it on himself. Then he chattered shrilly at Wombat. Mouse's agitated pink nose stuck out of a hole in the hat.

"Wombat, don't you do it! Oh, what a disgrace!"

Wombat was beaming. "I think it would be fun. He only wants me to do his tricks, and he'll pretend to be the trainer. Dear ole monkey, isn't he clever!"

Mouse covered its eyes. It could not bear to look as Wombat did all Charlie's tricks, while Charlie, wearing the uniform coat, called out his orders.

Wombat enjoyed being a monkey. He even tried to climb a rope, but fell down on his back, and was carried out to the cheers of the crowd. The Head Man was not pleased.

"I want *you* to be the trainer, and Charlie to do the tricks! I don't want any mix-ups!"

"Wombat is rather muddle-headed," explained Mouse.

"Too muddle-headed for me," said the Head Man. "Off you go. On your way."

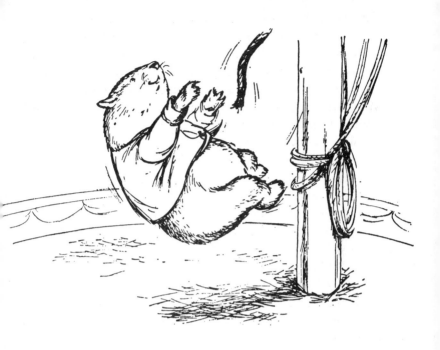

"You mean you don't want us to work in the circus any more?" quavered poor Mouse.

"No. You cause too many muddles. But your friend Tabby can stay."

Tabby stalked in, very grand in his uniform. Mouse ran to him and clung to his skinny, grey ankle.

"Tabby, Tabby, we've got to go away. They don't want us here any more."

"One for all and all for one," said Tabby grandly. "I shall leave too."

The Head Man didn't care, but the Lioness did. She was heart-broken to think that her tabby cub was going away. She wouldn't eat. She moped in her bed of straw. She cried big lion's tears.

"I don't know how I'll leave her," said Tabby sadly. "She's such a lonely old lioness."

Mouse pulled softly at his toenail.

"How much money have we got, Tabby?"

They counted it all up. They had the five pounds they had won with the photograph of "The Wonderful Womcat," and they had another three pounds the Head Man had given Tabby for being a lion tamer. It was just enough for a bike with red wheels.

"I was thinking," said Mouse. "I was thinking that if we bought Mrs Lion a nice, cuddly, furry toy, it might keep her company."

"Of course then we won't have enough money for our bike," said Wombat, "but we can go on saving up, can't we?"

So they bought a big, beautiful toy. It was a baby lion, with green eyes, and it was almost as big as Wombat.

The Lioness was delighted with it.

"It's really nicer than you," she told Tabby, "because it won't order me around and make me do tricks."

"There, I told you," said Tabby. "Nobody loves me, not *really*."

Wombat and Mouse were glad the old Lioness was happy now, but Tabby was sad.

"I feel so ordinary," he sighed.

"Then let's cheer ourselves up," said Mouse. "Let's go to the puppet show."

"Will there be free sardines?" asked Tabby eagerly.

Mouse thought not, but it said it was sure its friends would enjoy the puppet show just the same. And they did.

CHAPTER V

The Shiny Red Bike

TABBY CAT liked the puppets. So did Mouse. Everyone likes to see the funny little wooden people dancing and walking and squabbling on the ends of their strings. But Wombat simply loved them. He talked about nothing else.

"Mouse," he said, "I've got a horribubbly good idea. Mouse, you're not listening."

"Yes I am, Wombat dear."

"Then why are your ears pointing the other way? Eh?"

"To keep the wind out of them, Wombat dear," said little Mouse patiently.

"Wait till you hear my horribubbly good idea, you animals."

"We *are* waiting, muddle-head!" cried Tabby impatiently.

Wombat stuck his lip out. For a moment he thought he mightn't tell them, especially Tabby, who thought himself so grand. But the idea was too good to keep to himself.

"Let's have our own puppet show and go around the country earning lots of money! We'd have our bike with red wheels in no time."

Tabby at once wanted to know how they would buy the puppets, and who would work them, and why he had to have such a muddle-headed wombat for a friend when he was so handsome and wonderful a cat. Wombat just lay down and kicked his stout legs with joy.

"One of us can be a puppet! Hooray, I had a horribubbly good idea all by myself!"

Mouse bounced a bit with excitement. "You mean one of us could pretend, and have strings tied here and there, and all the time be a real, live animal? Oh, Wombat, you are clever!"

Wombat was modest. "The thought just came along, and I thunk it."

"But who's going to be the puppet?" asked Tabby.

"Me!"

"No, Wombat, your legs are much too short. You don't have any knees and all puppets have knees."

Wombat looked sadly at his legs. They *did* look fat and short and knee-less, more like furry brown sausages than anything else. Mouse didn't want its dear friend to be disappointed, so it chirruped:

"But don't you see, Wombat, if Tabby is the puppet, you can work the strings."

"I'll make him turn flips and jump backwards and fall over with a bang and everything!" Wombat was delighted.

"Oh, no, you won't," screeched Tabby. "Every time Wombat comes near me something awful happens! I won't be a puppet, I won't, I'm too delicate!"

Mouse stroked his paw. "What a shame!" It gave a sad sigh. "With your graceful legs, and your pretty tail, and everything. I was thinking of you as a ballet cat, really, you know, Tabby dear, but never mind."

A ballet cat! Tabby sleeked down his fur and coiled his tail around his paws and thought of himself flitting across the stage in a shiny tunic and black tights. It was such a beautiful picture!

"And you could be a ballet mouse, Mouse, with a little frilly skirt and a star between your ears. But how could Wombat manage the strings of two puppets?"

"I'll hold Mouse with my front paws and you with my back paws," promised Wombat.

"No, no, don't let him, Mouse. Something frightful will happen to dear old me!"

But Mouse explained that Wombat would be only pretending to work the strings, so nothing very bad could happen to poor Tabby.

Tabby and Mouse had a very busy morning. Wombat wasn't very helpful because he was worn out from so much thinking of clever thoughts, and went to sleep. He was delighted when he awakened and saw Mouse twirling around in a mouse-sized, pink, frilly skirt. Tabby also looked very remarkable as he flitted from place to place, putting his tail into graceful ballet positions.

"Doesn't he look like a teapot!" said Wombat admiringly. Tabby threw himself on the ground and kicked and cater-wauled until Wombat apologised and promised that he would make the puppet theatre. He did this by making a big box with no front side. It had red curtains in the front . . . Mouse made those . . . and a black curtain at the back. Mouse made that, too. Wombat stood at the back of the box and pretended to pull the strings of the puppets. The show looked very life-like. They set it up on the corner of a street in the town, and very soon a crowd of children and grown-ups had gathered around it.

Wombat liked boys and girls. He stood there beaming at them, and then he pulled his hat over his face and popped out from under it, and beamed again and made them all laugh. Something nipped his ankle, and he looked down to see Mouse pinching away, its nose pink with temper.

"Make the announcement!" hissed Mouse.

"Oh," said Wombat. "Forgot. Excuse me, everyone. Got to announce the Show. Wombat's Poppet Show! I mean puppet. But Mouse *is* a poppet puppet."

The curtains rattled aside, and there was Mouse, standing as stiffly as a little wooden Mouse in the middle of the stage. Mouse had strings attached to its back, and its four paws, and these Wombat held in one paddy paw. Mouse stared straight ahead and did its best to look like a real puppet.

"Now," said Wombat in a big whisper to the boys and girls, "when I pull the strings, this puppet will dance. If you hear someone whistling, that will be me, and you may clap if you like. Off I go!"

As Wombat whistled, Mouse lifted one foot and stood on the toe. Then it stood on the other toe. Everyone clapped. Some of the boys joined in with Wombat's whistle. Mouse popped up into the air and crossed its ankles in the smartest way. It twirled on the end of its long tail like a top. Then it tippy-toed across the stage, whirled around six times without coming down to earth, and sank to the floor in a bow.

Everyone loved Mouse. They clapped and clapped so loudly that Wombat had to say: "You be quiet now, children. We've got another puppet, and his name is Tabby. It's his turn now."

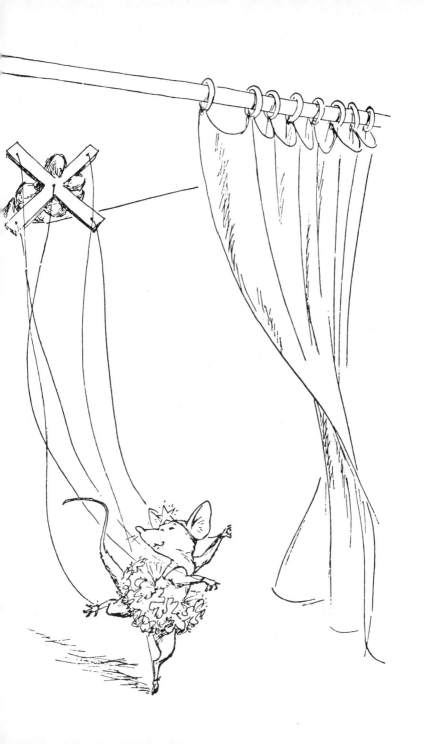

And Tabby, looking very fine in his tights and tunic, bounded on to the stage. Wombat smiled tenderly down at him.

"I know you want to be a success like Mouse, ole Tab, so I'll help!"

Wombat jerked on the string which held Tabby's tail, and at once Tabby rose into the air, head downwards.

"Whatever are you doing, you bad Wombat?" wailed Mouse, behind the scenes.

"I'm helping dear ole Tab to be a success, Mouse. You just watch. I do love helping, Mouse."

Tabby slowly came down to the floor again. This time he was determined not to leave it, and he hooked out his claws and stuck them into the wood of the stage. He clung there growling under his breath.

"Let *go*, Tabby!" said Wombat crossly, shaking Tabby with all his might. He tugged hard on the string tied around Tabby's middle, and Tabby's middle went up in the air like a hump. Wailing pitifully, Tabby had to let go. Wombat beamed at him.

"Now you're going to do a high kick, Tab."

Wombat jerked on the string attached to Tabby's ankles. One paw flew up over his head. The other paw flew up. Tabby looked as though he were swimming. The boys and girls simply loved it. They roared with laughter as Tabby whizzed across the stage and slowly rose out of sight tail first.

The children clapped and clapped. Wombat cried: "They love you so much they want you back again, lucky Tab!"

He let Tabby down, crash in the middle of the stage.

Tabby was so exhausted he hung from the strings like a cat made of straw and stuffing. So Wombat made him bow. It was a pity he dropped him on his nose in the middle of it. Then Tabby walked off on his front paws, with his tail sticking up like a flag. The children clapped and clapped again. Tabby was certainly a success.

"Oh, Tabby," giggled Mouse, "I've never laughed so much in all my mousy life."

"Tomorrow," said Tabby bitterly, "you'll be laughing on the other side of your whiskers, Miss Mouse. Oh, the shame of it all!"

Now that the show was over, Wombat closed the curtains. Mouse sat on the floor of the stage counting all the money the children and the grown-ups had thrown there. There was such a lot. The pile was much higher than Mouse, and almost half as high as Tabby, who sat there glaring and miaowling under his breath and untying the strings from his legs and tail.

"I'm leaving, you animals! I've had enough! I won't put up with it any more!"

"But you're our friend," said Wombat. "Aw, come on, Tabby, wasn't it fun, treely ruly?"

But Tabby wouldn't speak to them. And in the morning they found that he had gone, and so had all the money they had saved for the bike with red wheels. Mouse and Wombat didn't mind about the money, but they were very unhappy about Tabby.

"Perhaps I shouldn't have pulled him up into the air by his tail, Mouse."

"Cats like to be dignified. Oh, bother, bother, bother," said little Mouse, crying into a handkerchief the size of a five-penny stamp.

"I *love* ole Tab," gulped Wombat. "I didn't at first, but now I do. I love his funny face and his skinny old tail, and the way he thinks he's so handsome."

"Things won't be the same without a cat around," sobbed Mouse.

Just then there was a tremendous ting-a-ling outside the hedge where Mouse and Wombat had made their bed for the night.

"That sounds like . . ."

"A bike!"

They hurried around to the road. There was the shiniest, newest bike in the world. Never had wheels been so red,—red as roses, red as radishes!

There was a carrier on the back, and a tool-kit, and a pump, and a beautiful bell!

And riding this wonderful bike was Tabby Cat. He rang the bell again.

"Hurry up, you animals, don't you want to ride off and have adventures?"

"Tabby, you *didn't* run away!" said Wombat.

"You just went off to buy this lovely bike," said little Mouse.

Tabby looked conceited. "I was going to run away, and then I thought: how would Wombat and Mouse get on without their second-best friend? It's not everyone who has a friend like wonderful me!"

Wombat and Mouse said that was so. Tabby got into the carrier, Wombat sat on the seat and did the pedalling. Mouse sat on the handlebars and ring-a-dinged the bell. They pedalled off down the road to look for more adventures.

The
Muddle-headed
Wombat
at School

CHAPTER I

A Cat Needs Clever Friends

Mouse and Tabby Cat and Wombat lived in a little house at the edge of Big Bush. Big Bush was green and quiet and airy, and the right place for animals to live. Mouse was a kind, pretty Mouse who looked after the cooking and mousework and tried to bring Wombat up the right way. Tabby was a skinny grey cat who believed he was very handsome and brainy.

As for Wombat, he was just happy and muddle-headed.

Sometimes Tabby became discontented.

"You know, Mouse," he said, "a brilliant cat like me should have smart friends; people who can count to more than four."

"I can count to more than four," answered Mouse, very offended. "And I can do hard sums, and I know geography and history, and I can knit and . . ."

"Yes, Mouse," sighed Tabby, "but you're so small you're hardly noticed."

Mouse was very upset about Tabby's remark, because, after all, it couldn't help being small, and it made the best of things. So, giving a small fairy sob, it dived into a lily and pulled the petals in after itself. But it came out very quickly indeed, with a bee after it.

"You see, Mouse," explained Tabby, "even a bee is as big as a dragon to *you*. Anyway, I wasn't talking about you. I was talking about Wombat."

"It's not Wombat's fault he can only count up to four," said Mouse, feeling very grey and miserable by now. "He runs out of paws, that's the trouble."

"Just the same," said Tabby, "your handsome pussy needs clever friends. He needs Conversations."

By this time Mouse needed its warm brown comfortable wombat friend very much indeed. But where was Wombat?

"Down on the rubbish tip, *that's* where that animal is," said Tabby, and he was right. The rubbish tip was a little gully near Big Bush where people, humans and animals, often put unwanted things. Wombat loved to poke around there and find useful old saucepan lids (for banging) and worn-out motor-tyres (for bowling). But this afternoon he had found something really exciting. He lay on the ground and kicked his stout legs with joy. He made such loud, wombatty noises that Tabby and Mouse came running at once.

"Oh, Wombat, did you see a snake?" gasped little Mouse.

"Did you get a prickle in your paw? Say you have!" begged Tabby, who loved playing doctors.

"I'm just happy," said Wombat. "Look what I've found!"

Tabby and Mouse looked. Tabby shuddered; he was such a fine, delicate cat. Wombat had found an old, old teddybear, bald all over, with no nose, only one leg, and mean little glassy eyes. Mouse *was* cross.

"Throw away that dirty old thing at once! You wombat, you!"

Wombat stroked the teddy's bare, cottony old head. "Don't you take any notice of Mouse, Tedda. It's such an excitabubble little animal."

"Why do you call him Tedda?" asked Tabby.

"Because he's a teddabear of course," said Wombat. "Even a wombat can see *that*."

69

No matter how much Mouse pointed out that Tedda was grubby and raggy and old, Wombat wouldn't listen. No matter how haughtily Tabby switched his tail, Wombat paid no attention. He chatted to Tedda all the way home.

"If Mouse says anything horribubble to you, such as having a good wash in soap and water, we'll put Mouse right in the sugar basin, with the lid on."

"Well, let me sew up his poor old leg!" pleaded Mouse, who thought that once it got Tedda away from Wombat it could easily give him a quick bath. But Wombat was stern.

"Tedda doesn't like needles stuck in him, do you, Tedda?"

He gave Tedda a loving poke in the stomach, expecting that he would squeak like all teddybears. But Tedda didn't say a word. His squeaker had been broken years before. A tear rolled down Wombat's leathery nose.

"I do believe my Tedda's been hurt, treely ruly!"

"Leave it to your clever Tabby!" said Tabby importantly. "I can buy a new squeaker at the toyshop, and we shall have a lovely, exciting operation. I shall be Doctor Tabby!"

"You might hurt my friend Tedda, you old cat!" growled Wombat, and he stuffed the bear down the front of his cardigan, glared at Tabby, and trundled off. Mouse felt just a little jealous. After all, it had always been Wombat's very best friend.

"Perhaps you are right, Tabby dear," it said thoughtfully. "Perhaps Wombat should go to school and learn things, and then we could all have Conversations."

Besides, thought Mouse, school would get Wombat away from that horrid old Tedda.

Wombat was thrilled when Tabby and Mouse told him about school. They made it sound very exciting.

"You'll learn all kinds of interesting things, Wombat," said Tabby, who had been to school before when he was younger, "such as drawing on the blackboard, and singing, and exercises, and sums."

"And the Teacher will tell you lovely stories," added Mouse.

Wombat drummed his back paws on the floor excitedly. "Will she tell me my treely ruly favourites. . . . Cindagorilla and the Lizard of Oz?"

"Oh, yes," promised Mouse. "And, besides, think of all the people you'll have to play with, wallabies and bandicoots and jew lizards, and even boy and girl joeys."

Wombat loved boy and girl joeys. He made up his mind right away.

"I'll start tomorrow!" he roared. "And Tedda will go too!"

Tabby was shocked. "Oh, no, he's much too grubby for school, ugh!"

"Teacher wouldn't think he's respectable," said Mouse.

"He is so respectabubble!" growled Wombat, and he pulled his hat over his eyes and wouldn't come out, but stayed there muttering things like: "I won't go to school if Tedda can't go too!"

Tabby twitched a meaning whisker at Mouse. "We shall have to have a tiny talk, I'm afraid, Mouse."

So Tabby and Mouse had a little talk. They agreed that if Wombat said Tedda could have a good bath, they would allow him to go to school with Wombat.

"And to make things easier," said Tabby, "I shall go along too, as a friend of the family, and explain that Wombat is not only just a little muddle-headed, but that he is very attached to this dreadful teddybear."

"Oh, Tabby, you ARE wonderful," said grateful Mouse.

"I know," said Tabby.

It took a long time for Mouse to persuade Wombat to allow his Tedda to be washed.

"Don't be mean, Wombat," said clever Mouse. "After all, wouldn't Tedda enjoy school, too? Perhaps he'd like to hear Cinderella."

"Aw right," said Wombat cheerfully. "And what do you think, Mouse? I took the squeaker out of my old sick-dog and Tedda ate it for me and now he squeaks."

72

"Oh, my!" said Mouse. The sick-dog was a squashy woollen dog that Wombat liked to take to bed when he was feeling miserable. However, it hadn't a squeaker, it had a barker. True enough, Tedda now barked, ark-ark! Mouse felt this wasn't right at all.

"Well," it said in a hopeless kind of way, "I'll wash Tedda and perhaps he'll look better."

All the time Tedda was being washed Wombat thumped around giving directions.

"Don't get soap in his dear little beady eyes! Watch out for his poor ear, it's terribubbly loose! I'm here, Tedda, don't be frightened. You just tell me if Mouse hurts you and I'll sit on it."

Tedda came out of the basin looking very soggy and flat, but Mouse said that as soon as he was dry he would be as fluffy as a bald teddybear could be. Mouse pegged him on the line, and Wombat sat on the grass and told him what great fun they would have at school.

· "We're going to learn things like four and eight make eleventy one, and C O W spells cat, and things like that!"

"And perhaps you'll be allowed to play in the sandpit," said Tabby.

"Yes, we'll play in the sandpip, Tedda," said Wombat. "What's a sandpip, eh, Tabby, eh?"

So Tabby explained. Wombat thought this was very splendid, for wombats are digging animals and he loved to dig.

"I'll dig a tunnel eleventy miles long, and you and the other children can play in it, Tedda," he said.

Mouse was rather sad. Though it busied itself washing Wombat's cardigan, and doing other little jobs, its glasses misted over now and then.

"How I shall miss you, Wombat. Even though you'll become very clever, I'll miss you."

"I'll pretend to be muddle-headed while I'm with you, Mouse," promised Wombat.

At last Tedda was dry. Although he had no nose and only one leg, he was now a pretty golden colour and Mouse knew he would have no germs on him. Wombat was delighted. "Teacher will love Tedda best of all," he said.

The next morning Tabby and Wombat got ready. Mouse saw that Wombat washed his ears, and Tabby cut his toenails, which tired him very much. He said it was like trying to trim a hedge and he was too delicate, really.

Then Mouse and Tabby gave Wombat's thick brown coat a good brushing with the little straw whisk broom, and Mouse tidied up his clean cardigan, and he was ready.

As it was the beginning of term, lots of people were enrolling. Some of the younger bandicoots were already missing their mothers and crying very hard. Tabby thought it might be a good idea for Wombat to show them his Tedda and take their minds off their troubles.

"I'll enrol you, Wombat," he said helpfully. "Besides, I know Teacher will be delighted to see *me*."

Tabby was looking very spruce in a new red waistcoat and bow tie. He had practised a lot of big words to show the Teacher that even though he had a muddle-headed wombat for a friend, he was truly a very well-educated cat. The Teacher was a lady kangaroo called Miss Roo.

Tabby took charge of things at once. "Of course," he explained, "wombats are *different*. I don't know what they have in their heads, dust, I suppose, and old fish bones, and peachstones. Things like that. I don't suppose my Wombat will ever get out of First Class, poor fellow. But we must TRY to teach him something."

Miss Roo understood. She also understood about Tedda.

"But Tedda is allowed to come only for a week or two," she said. "The other pupils might think Wombat a baby, and he wouldn't like that. Now, put your name right here, Tabby."

Tabby wrote his name in his best paw-writing. Even though it was a very ordinary name, it looked very fine. Tabby felt wonderfully important.

"Splendid," said Miss Roo. "Now you're enrolled. I've put you into Third Class, as you're so clever."

"But I don't want to go to school," gurgled Tabby. "I just wanted to enrol Wombat!"

"You don't want to go to school, a clever cat like you?" cried Miss Roo. She seemed so surprised and disappointed that Tabby didn't know what to say. He didn't want to offend Miss Roo, but on the other hand he didn't want to go back to school either.

"You could be so helpful, you see, Tabby," said Miss Roo. "You could be blackboard cat, in charge of the chalk. I DO need a reliable person to do that, you know."

At once Tabby saw himself handing out beautiful sticks of blue and yellow chalk, and smacking on the paw any cheeky wallaby or bandicoot who grabbed. It was a lovely picture.

"Well," he said, "in that case . . . I mean, just to be helpful . . . I was brought up to be a helpful pussy, you know . . . perhaps just for a little while. But now I'd better go and fetch Wombat."

But Wombat wasn't anywhere in the playground. A saucy young bandicoot had been rude to Tedda, and Wombat had marched right home. Poor Mouse was sitting on the edge of the teapot explaining to Wombat all the reasons why he just had to go to school now that Tabby had taken all the trouble to enrol him.

"Won't," said Wombat. He lay on the ground and waved his legs in the air. He felt happy and carefree with no more worries. "Won't, and Tedda won't either."

"I don't care about Tedda!" cried Mouse. "I don't care if he has nothing but sawdust in his head for ever and ever. But you're my Wombat!"

Just then Tabby rushed home, fur on end, whiskers twitching.

"I'm enrolled and Wombat isn't!" he cried. "It's not fair, Mouse, you know. I'm not the muddle-head in this family. Oh, how did it happen? Everything happens to me!"

CHAPTER II

The Beautiful School Tie

THE next day Tabby prowled off to school. He was very sulky, and would not eat his breakfast, even though Mouse had risen early to make him a special sardine sandwich. Mouse *was* sorry that their splendid plan had gone wrong. It wiped away a tear with the end of its tail.

"Oh, very well, Mouse!" snapped Tabby. "I'll eat it just to please you." And he choked down half his sandwich.

"Oh, Wombat, please won't you go to school with dear kind Tabby?" begged Mouse, banging Tabby on the back.

"Naow. Won't," said Wombat.

"You'll be sorry!" gasped Tabby. But he didn't really believe it, and neither did Wombat, who went out into the garden and lay on his back in the sunshine and ate a buttercup in a doleful way. Tedda didn't say anything. He just sat on Wombat's round, football-shaped stomach and slid off every now and then.

But when Tabby came home that afternoon, things were quite different. For one thing, school ties had been given out. Tabby had such a scraggy little neck that the tie went round three times. But still, it was a school tie, striped red and yellow. Wombat had never seen anything so important.

"It's just like a terribubbly nice caterpillar!" he cried. "Oh, why can't I have one like that, Mouse, eh? Why?"

"Only school pupils have school ties," said Mouse stiffly, because it was cross with Wombat.

"And I'm a school pupil," said Tabby smugly. "Now I must do my homework."

"First I'll make you some hot milk and a fish sandwich, Tabby dear," said Mouse. "You must keep your strength up."

Wombat waited, bright-eyed. But there was no little snack for him. Mouse said he could go and eat some more buttercups for all it cared.

"And you're not to bother Tabby, you hear, you wombat you? He's busy."

"Oh, yes, I am," said Tabby proudly. "Oh, I *am* a busy pussy. I have to draw a cow, and then I have to cut some coloured paper into special shapes, and then I must do my spelling. I'll do my spelling first because it's the hardest."

And Tabby printed, very carefully, B O Y, and D O G, and C A T. Wombat looked on enviously.

"I'm going to be the best cat in the school," boasted Tabby. "Miss Roo will be so pleased with her handsome pussy. And after I have been blackboard cat for a while, she's promised I can be traffic cat and have a red flag and lead the children across the street at the crossing."

This was too much for Wombat, who was almost bursting with jealousy.

"You won't, you won't!" he roared, jumping up and down with rage. Every time he jumped, Tedda said 'Ark-ark!" in a surprised way. Mouse scampered in and gave them both a frightful glare.

"You stop bothering Tabby!" it squeaked, "or you'll get such a bite on the toe!"

Wombat stopped to draw breath, and Tabby said quickly: "And today Miss Roo read us all a story called the Uglv Duckling. It was all about a poor ugly duckling who grew up to be a beautiful swan. Oh, it was *beautiful!*"

Sadly Wombat followed Mouse out to the kitchen. Wombat hadn't had a happy day. He missed Tabby, and he didn't like his little Mouse being sad and disappointed and quiet. "Why can't I have a school tie like a horribubbly nice red and yellow worm? And why can't I hear stories bout ugly dumplings that grow up to be beautiful scones?"

"Because you don't go to school, silly," said Mouse.

"I can't go to school if people are rude to Tedda," explained Wombat. "And that bandicoot was rude. He said teddas don't bark."

"That awful tedda does," said Mouse. It gave Tedda a little thump and Tedda said "Ark-ark!"

"You don't like Tedda either," said Wombat sadly. "And he's just so loverly."

Because he wasn't feeling happy, Wombat became hard to get on with.

"I'm going out to find myself some centipedes."

"Wombat!" squeaked Mouse. "I won't allow you to eat centipedes."

"Not going to eat them. Too tickly with all those legs and everything. Going to put them on Tabby Cat. Then he might let me try on his school tie."

"Don't you dare!" cried Mouse.

"You like Tabby betterer than me, I do believe," said Wombat sorrowfully, "just because he goes to school."

Still he was very interested in all that Tabby was doing. He sat and watched him doing his homework. Now Tabby was cutting out some squares and triangles in bright coloured paper. His tongue stuck out like a little end of pink ribbon, and he was very careful to cut straight.

"Tabby, why do you have to have a tie?"

"To tie round my neck, muddle-head. Don't interrupt."

"Why, is your neck loose?" asked Wombat. "It *looks* loose."

Tabby gave him a scornful look. But just then Wombat leaned across and put his stout flat paw on Tabby's homework. It left a huge, muddy mark.

"You've spoiled my beautiful spelling!" screamed Tabby. "Oh, what's the use of being a cat? Nobody cares about a cat, *really*."

Wombat was ashamed. "I'm terribubbly sorry, Tabby," he said humbly. "I thought I had a clean paw. I'm sure I remember licking it. . . . I'm a nasty Wombat, Tabby, treely ruly."

He felt so bad he went to see Mouse. "I've been an awful Wombat to my dear second-best friend, Mouse, so I'm going to make him a wonderful surprise."

Mouse smiled for the first time that day. "That sounds more like my very own Wombat."

"I'm going to make him a lunch box. And you can write his name on it, Mouse. B A T . . . Tab."

Mouse was so delighted it hugged Wombat's ankle. It helped him find the hammer and some tacks.

"I'll call you when I'm ready, Mouse."

So Mouse finished cooking supper, and made a cake (fish-flavoured for Tabby) and washed its face and paws and tidied up its tiny pink apron, and waited to be called. And, long after the sun had gone down, Wombat called it.

Mouse hurried outside, smiling proudly.

There was Wombat standing beside a huge box, half as big as himself.

"My!" whispered Mouse.

"I knew you'd like it," said Wombat. "Look at all the nails."

"Isn't it just a teeny bit big, Wombat dear?"

"I made it big so that Tabby could put hundreds of fish sandwiches in it. He'll be pleased, won't he, Mouse? He'll beam all over his hidjus little face, won't he, Mouse, eh?"

Tabby wandered outside. He had done his spelling homework all over again, and he was a happy, contented cat.

"Whatever's THAT?"

"It's your lunch box, Tabby dear," said Mouse timidly, "Wombat made it for you."

"Because I'm treely ruly sorry for being such a horri-bubble Wombat and making paw prints on your home-work, Tab," added Wombat.

Tabby stood by the lunch box. It came up to his left ear. He knew he would never be able to lift it by himself. But he showed he was a kind and noble cat, even though he *was* scraggy.

"It's just the most wonderful box I ever, ever had, Wombat!"

Wombat beamed with joy. "And Mouse is going to write your name on it. B A T . . . Tab."

Not even that made Tabby screech. He smiled and said: "But Wombat, not for a lunch box. Imagine if one of those saucy bandicoots scribbled on it, just imagine! Oh, no, I want to keep it at home for my treasure box."

"Oh, Tabby," said Mouse admiringly.

"I'll keep my coloured pencils in it, and my Christmas hanky with Santa Claus in the corner and my homework that Miss Roo has marked with a star . . . oh, it will be useful, Wombat! Thank you so much!"

Wombat was delighted. He thought he would give Tabby another lovely surprise.

"And I've decided to go to school with you, Tab. Tedda and I squawked it over and Tedda says that if that bandicoot is rude to him again all I'll have to do is to sit on that bandicoot and squash it like a pancake."

Mouse sighed. "I'm sure Teacher wouldn't like pupils looking like pancakes. Perhaps I'd better come along and keep an eye on you, Wombat."

"But you're so clever already, Mouse!" said Tabby, who rather feared Mouse might become traffic mouse instead of him.

"No, I've made up my mind," said Mouse. So it helped Wombat and Tabby carry the treasure box inside, and they had a happy evening putting away Tabby's treasures.

Next day Miss Roo was very surprised to see that she had two new pupils. She could see at once by Mouse's flashing spectacles and wonderfully clean toenails that here would be a very useful pupil indeed.

Wombat liked Miss Roo. He was pleased to see that she kept spare rubbers and pencils and a hanky in her pouch, just as though it were a real pocket.

"I do like your wiggly nose," he told her. "And you've got pretty brown eyes and a tremendous tail. I'm glad you're my teacher, aren't I, Mouse?"

Mouse thought Wombat had very bad manners, but Miss Roo didn't mind. "I hear you can count to four, Wombat. Count for me."

"No, too tired," said Wombat.

Mouse gave him a sharp pinch. "Do what you're told, Wombat. You're at school now."

"Tell me how many paws you have," said Miss Roo kindly.

Wombat beamed. "I've got two on this end and two on that end. Aw, where are the two on that end, Mouse? They've gone!"

"You're standing on them," said Mouse, pink with shame.

"Well, that's four paws, isn't it," said Miss Roo. "How many ears have you?"

"Three!" said Wombat.

"Oh, Miss Roo," said poor Mouse. "He's been awful today."

"And how many heads, Wombat?" asked Miss Roo.

"I've forgotten."

But Miss Roo seemed to be used to wombats or other muddle-heads.

"Then we won't have any more counting today. If you'd like to draw on the blackboard, you may go and get some coloured chalk from Tabby Cat."

Tabby made a big important fuss about opening the chalk box and choosing three sticks of chalk for Wombat.

"While you're drawing awful old things, Mouse and I will be doing terribly hard sums," he boasted. Wombat didn't mind.

"I'm going to draw a train and Miss Roo, and then I'll draw *you*, Tab," he promised. Tedda sat by and watched, barking now and then when Wombat accidentally bumped him in the stomach.

But somehow the train looked like a snake, and the picture of Miss 'Roo wouldn't turn out right. Wombat thought he'd draw Tabby.

He drew Tabby's long neck, and his skinny little legs and his knotty tail. Tabby himself was very eager to see the drawing, which he thought would be very flattering and handsome. As soon as he had finished his arithmetic, he asked permission of Miss Roo to look at the drawing. He turned pale grey with rage.

"That's not me!" he screamed. "It looks like a sick lizard. Oh, what have you done with my whiskers and my elegant little paws?"

He was so upset he flew up the long red curtain at the window and sat on the pole at the top, sobbing, and refusing to come down.

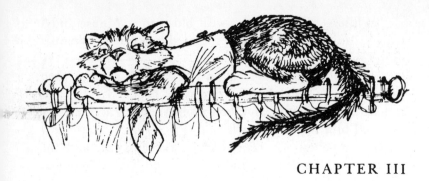

CHAPTER III

Teddas Love Dogs

WHEN Tabby Cat became so upset, all the other new pupils became worried, too. Some shrieked for their mothers. Some raced around the room. One small wallaby jumped into Miss Roo's pouch and wouldn't come out. There was a fearful noise of squeaking and wailing and stamping. While Miss Roo was trying to quieten the class, Mouse scampered over to look at the picture of Tabby which had caused all the fuss.

"Oh, Wombat!" cried Mouse, "no wonder Tabby is crying. It's such an ugly picture!"

"It is not ugerly!" growled Wombat. "Look at his pretty blue nose!"

"I haven't a blue nose!" shrieked Tabby. "Even on a cold day my nose never goes blue."

"Why is my picture ugerly then?" demanded Wombat. "Just because it has green ears, I suppose. Just because its tail got a kink in it accidentabubbly."

"You rub that picture out!" ordered Mouse. "Stop crying, Tabby dear. Wombat will rub it out, won't you, Wombat?"

"Won't!" roared Wombat.

"You rub that picture out, or I'll . . . I'll bite Tedda!" cried Mouse desperately.

Then Wombat did a very awful thing. He grabbed Mouse and rubbed the picture out with it. Mouse made a very good blackboard duster because it was so plump and velvety. But you can imagine how many colours Mouse was when Wombat put it on the floor at last. Miss Roo ran to help, but she was too late.

"I'm green and blue and purple all over!" sobbed Mouse.

"You're a very naughty Wombat!" said Miss Roo. "Go outside for the rest of the lesson!"

Wombat didn't want to do that, for he was enjoying school so much. But he was sorry he had made Tabby run up the curtain, and Mouse cry, and Miss Roo angry with him. He didn't know what to do, so he ate the chalk. Down it went, first the purple, then the blue.

"I won't eat the green, though," said Wombat, "it might taste like spinach."

The pupils were so shocked they stopped squeaking and running about. Tabby toppled off the curtain and thumped on the floor. Mouse and Miss Roo stood as if frozen. Wombat looked timidly around. He couldn't quite make out why everyone was staring.

"I don't like spinach," he whispered.

"Outside with you!" said Miss Roo sternly. "Quick march! And you will not be allowed to go to the school picnic tomorrow."

Wombat picked up Tedda and gave him a sad, ashamed punch in the stomach. Tedda hooted out a wheezy bark which continued all the way outside because the barker had stuck. Miss Roo, who was very upset, said to Mouse:

"I do hope he won't be sick, Mouse. Imagine eating chalk!"

"Oh, Miss Roo," was all poor Mouse could say.

Meanwhile Tabby was groaning loudly, though he hadn't been hurt at all. He turned up his eyes and shivered his whiskers. He wanted attention. But Miss Roo was too worried about Wombat.

"He's the most muddle-headed animal I've ever had in my class. Is he always like that?"

Mouse nodded sorrowfully. "But please let him stay in school, dear Miss Roo. There must be something he can learn."

"Oh, what about poor wonderful me?" moaned Tabby.

"Stop your nonsense or you'll get a good smack!" snapped Miss Roo. "You know very well you're only pretending to be hurt. You go outside, too!"

Tabby marched out, crossly switching his tail. Wombat was sitting on the step slapping Tedda.

"Don't you bark at me, you wicked Teddabear!"

"If you didn't touch his tummy he wouldn't bark, you great muddle-head!" squalled Tabby.

"I didn't touch his hidjus tummy! He's just doing it to annoy!" said Wombat.

"If it wasn't for that raggy old bear I'd still be Miss Roo's useful pupil," said Tabby bitterly.

And Tabby snatched Tedda from Wombat and flung him, still barking, over the school fence.

The moment Tedda landed he was whipped up by a large black dog who had been waiting patiently there till lunch time. Often he was given scraps and crusts from the school lunches. He thought of himself as the school dog. Now, however, something exciting and unusual had come his way. He rushed off into the long grass with Tedda. By the time Wombat reached the fence there was no sign of dog or bear. But Wombat could see large dog tracks in the sand.

"A dog's run off with Tedda!" he roared. "My bestest bear!"

Tabby was very upset. He hadn't meant Tedda to be lost for ever.

"Do dogs eat bears?" cried Wombat. He was so worried he didn't notice that playtime bell had rung. There were now lots of pupils in the playground, as well as Miss Roo, who was keeping an eye on them.

"Oh, Miss Roo," said Tabby unhappily. "Your lovely pussy has done a dreadful thing. I threw Tedda over the fence, and a dog took him!"

Miss Roo was very disappointed in her new pupils. "Really, Tabby, you will have to be punished. You can stay home from the school picnic tomorrow, as well!"

Wombat gave a huge sob. He was very disappointed. Mouse put its kind little pink paw into his. Its glasses glittered earnestly.

"If Wombat promises never to eat any more chalk, and Tabby Cat promises to go and fetch Tedda back, won't you let them go to the picnic? please, dear Teacher."

"I might," said Miss Roo.

Mouse called Tabby and Wombat together. It spoke sternly: "Now, you animals, you must try to be good. You don't want to miss a bush picnic, with barbecued sausages and everything, do you?"

Tabby and Wombat, who loved each other very much, were only too ready to make friends. In fact, after Tabby had wriggled out of Wombat's forgiving hug, he felt very much thinner and taller than usual. But before he could complain, Mouse went briskly on:

"I have a plan. We shall all go to that dog's kennel, and Wombat shall stand outside and call him names."

"And then he'll come rushing out to bite you, Wombat!" added Tabby eagerly. He was still feeling himself for bruises.

"And then you can sit on him, Wombat," went on Mouse, "while Tabby and I go into the kennel and rescue Tedda."

Wombat thought this was a wonderful idea. But he felt Tabby should do the name-calling.

"Me?" cried Tabby. "Poor frail little me? Besides, I couldn't think of anything. I'm too well-brought-up."

It was agreed that Tabby was the best skinny animal
to creep into the kennel, and Wombat was the best fat
animal for sitting on a dog. So they decided to try Mouse's
plan.

The dog lived in a very rich kennel with a red peaked
roof, a nameplate over the door saying PETE, and a little
chimney.

"My!" marvelled Mouse. "Does that dog have a fire-
place inside his kennel? I don't know what dogs are coming
to."

Tabby thought it was a pretend chimney.

"It's quite big enough for me to climb down and rescue
Tedda, you know, Mouse. And that's more exciting than
going in the door. Oh, I do think things are going to be
all right after all, and we'll be allowed to attend the picnic!"

Now all this time they could hear the dog thumping around in his kennel. Now and then one of his large black paws stuck out the door.

"I suppose he's playing with Tedda," said Wombat dolefully. "Eating him, I wouldn't be surprised."

"Then we must rescue him as soon as we can!" said Mouse bravely. "You creep around to the back of the kennel, Tabby dear, where you can pop down the chimney. You start calling names, Wombat. As for me, I shall get under this big leaf and be in no one's way."

Mouse smiled helpfully and flickered under a large dock leaf. Tabby, putting on a heroic look, crept around the back of the kennel.

Wombat tried his best to do his part.

"Hey, you nice old dog, I'm going to call you some awful names as soon as I can think of them."

"Call him a pussy cat!" prompted Mouse from under its dock leaf.

"Oh, yes!" beamed Wombat. "You're a pussy cat, dog! Well, not treely ruly. It's just an awful name Mouse told me to call you."

The dog hated cats and he was very insulted. Out he came like a rocket. He was a very large dog, much bigger than Wombat, with many more teeth.

"I'm going!" said Wombat sensibly. "Goodbye, everyone!"

And he trundled off in the opposite direction, with the dog snapping and snarling after him.

Mouse could scarcely believe its spectacles.

"Oh, what a cowardly custard! Oh, what a disgrace! After all I've done to bring that wombat up the right way!"

But meanwhile Tabby had climbed down the chimney of the dog's kennel. Lying at the bottom in the straw he found Tedda. He was grubby, but he had not been hurt. Tabby gave Tedda a sharp nip on the leg before he rescued him.

"This is all your fault!"

He dragged him out into the sunshine and looked around for praise. But Mouse was still stamping around with indignation.

"Did you see that Wombat, Tabby? He ran off and left me. His MOUSE! I might have been gobbled up by that dog. Oh, I shall never forgive him even if he IS muddle-headed."

99

Mouse and Tabby dragged Tedda a long way through the grass until they could see the kennel no longer. At last they saw Wombat trundling towards them, a very subdued Wombat who didn't quite look himself.

"Look, Wombat!" bragged Tabby. "I rescued Tedda. I was so brave, Wombat, you can't imagine. There aren't many cats like me, you know, bold as well as clever."

Wombat gave Tedda a sad little thump in the stomach. He didn't seem very pleased.

"Oh, Wombat," cried Mouse anxiously, forgetting how cross it was. "Did that horrid dog bite you?"

"No," said Wombat. Then he confessed. "Promise you'll never tell my terribubble secret, Mouse. Promise, Tab? Aw right then. That dog sat on me, just imaginabubble!"

Tabby thought it was very fair.

"Just think of the people you've sat on," he pointed out.

"Yes, but that's for wombats to do," said Wombat.

"Not *every* time," said Mouse sensibly. "Turn and turn about, *I* say."

But Wombat, although he was as rolypoly as ever, and not at all squashed, felt disgraced. He just hoped his Auntie Flannel, who had brought him up when he was a wombatlet, would never get to hear of it. Also, he didn't like Tedda very much any more. Mouse and Tabby saw this.

"I expect that poor dog is crying his eyes out because he hasn't a teddybear friend," Mouse said sadly.

"Poor lonely dog!" sighed Tabby. He rolled up his eyes. "A dog needs a friend."

"Perhaps he won't eat his lunch. He might fret himself to a shadow," added Mouse cunningly.

"Treely ruly?" asked Wombat, interested. "A shadow of what?"

"A dog, stupid!" snapped Mouse.

"All he needs is a Tedda of his own," said Tabby cleverly.

Wombat clasped Tedda jealously to his cardigan front. Even though he didn't love him any more, he didn't want to give him away.

He said he'd have to ask Tedda whether he wanted to go and live with the big black dog. There followed a rather one-sided conversation. Whenever Tedda barked, Wombat thumped him, so it was hard to tell what poor Tedda was trying to say. At last Wombat burst into tears.

"I do treely ruly believe he wants to go and live with that old dog!"

Mouse stroked his ankle tenderly.

"But Wombat," it said, very sensibly. "Perhaps Tedda likes the dog, too. He won't have to go to school . . . and I *do* think Miss Roo was upset by all that barking . . . and the dog will love him and cuddle up with him every night."

Wombat glared at Tedda.

"Well, suppose we go to the school picnic, and Tedda behaves himself very well, then will you let him go to live with the black dog?" coaxed Mouse.

"I might," said Wombat.

"Promise?" asked cunning Tabby. "Because if you don't, I'm going to draw a picture of you being sat on, and I'll draw it on the blackboard, too!"

Wombat said he promised.

CHAPTER IV

Picnic In Big Bush

AFTER Tabby had explained in a great many long words that he had rescued Tedda, and that he was truly sorry for throwing him away, and after Wombat had explained in a few short, ordinary words that although he hadn't been sick after eating the chalk he would never, never eat any again—Miss Roo forgave them both and said they could go to the Big Bush School Picnic.

Of course Wombat and Tabby had been to other picnics, but a school picnic is different. It is *important*.

Wombat beamed and Tabby danced.

"We'll be so good," cried Tabby. "And as I'm so very nice ordinarily, when I'm very good I'm an angel cat."

"And I'll do everything I'm told," promised Wombat. "Even if you tell me to climb a tree backwards, which is terribubbly hard, even for a possum."

"Very well," said kind Miss Roo.

That night Mouse had a serious talk with Wombat.

"I don't mean to get into muddles, Mouse," he said humbly. "How do you stay so sensibubble, Mouse, eh?"

"Because I'm a mouse."

"Then I'm going to grow up to be a mouse!" said Wombat.

"No," said Mouse. "But you can grow up into a sensible wombat, if you try."

Wombat thought for a while. He stood on his head and waved his stout legs. He was trying to think of something he could do well, but no thoughts would come.

"You can dig," said Mouse helpfully.

"And you can light a campfire, I can't imagine why," added Tabby, who wasn't good at that. Once he had set fire to his own whiskers, which put him off lighting campfires forever after.

Wombat fell over and kicked with joy.

"Maybe Teacher will let me light the campfire!"

Mouse made up its mind to ask. Wombat would so love to show everyone that there was one thing he could do without muddles.

Next day was a fine day. Birds were tossing in the blue sky. The gumleaves showed pink tips. When the wind blew all the bush threw back its arms like green wings.

"Oh, we will have a lovely time!" cried Mouse, blotting a drop of dew off its ear.

Each animal had to bring a special lunch, to be shared with everyone, and also pack some chops or sausages or tomatoes to grill over the campfire.

Mouse decided it would take sausages. Tabby carefully packed a basket, adding a tin of salmon for himself, in case he felt weak, some bread and peanut butter for Wombat, and a few grass seeds and two geranium petals for Mouse.

The friends hurried off to the edge of Big Bush, where they had to meet all the young wallabies and koalas and rabbits who attended the bush school. Miss Roo was there, too, looking calm and helpful, which is a good way for a teacher to look.

Wombat and Tabby, who were carrying the picnic basket between them, laughed with excitement. The sweet smells of damp earth and fallen leaves, the scratchy way the twigs moved against the sky, made them feel very happy.

Tedda was tied on Wombat's back.

"Anyone who feels tired can ride in my hat," offered Wombat.

"I'm tired!" said Mouse smartly, and it scampered up over Tedda and slipped into Wombat's hat.

"Off we go, children!" said Miss Roo, and she bounded up the track. The whole class hopped and waddled and trotted after her. Mouse lay back at ease on Wombat's bristly fur and peered out proudly through one of the holes in the hat.

"I *am* lucky to be travelling by taxi!" it chirruped.

"What about me?" complained Tabby. "My feet are getting wet, you know. I shall be sneezing tonight, you just see."

"I like muddy feet best," said Wombat.

After a while they came to a clearing made by a long-ago bushfire. It was full of sunshine, the trees stood in a ring around it, and in the grass were small blue flowers. The little animals were delighted. Here was just the right place for a picnic. Miss Roo thought so, too.

"The creek is near, so we can get water for our tea, and here are some good flat stones for our campfire. Now, who is good at lighting fires?"

"Wombat!" said Mouse, appearing pink and refreshed from Wombat's hat.

Miss Roo wasn't quite sure of that.

"Just because I couldn't remember how many ears I have, you think I'm muddle-headed at everything," said Wombat sadly. "And I'm very good at fires, treely ruly. I am horribubbly careful with matches, and if the fire won't burn, I have plenty of blow."

He showed how much blow he had. After they had rescued two or three of the smallest rabbits from the tops of bushes where they had been blown, Miss Roo said it looked as though Wombat should indeed light the campfire.

Tedda sat by, watching, while Wombat got to work. He lit the fire on a flat rock so that it wouldn't by any chance get away and set the scrub alight. He did it so well and carefully that Miss Roo said he might grill the chops and sausages too, while she took off the other pupils to play hide and seek in the bush. Mouse *was* proud of its Wombat.

Wombat was proud of himself, too.

"Now Miss Roo is thinking 'Well, perhaps he can't count, but he does grill a terribubbly tasty sausage.' "

Just then the sharp stick that was holding the sausages and chops burned through, and all the food fell into the fire. There was a tremendous sizzle. Tabby shot out of the scrub where he had been hiding, and pointed a trembling paw.

"What do you expect a poor hardworking cat to eat? Look at those sausages! Charred like little black sticks!"

"Wahhhhhh!" roared Wombat, heartbroken.

"Such a thing could happen to anyone, poor Wombat!" comforted Mouse.

"No, it could only happen to a wombat!" sobbed Wombat. He pulled his hat over his face and wouldn't come out, even when Miss Roo patted his paw and told him not to mind.

"We've so much other lunch!" she explained. "Don't worry, Wombat dear."

But Wombat would not be comforted. He had so wanted to show Teacher how good he was at lighting fires and cooking sausages. He sat by himself and was miserable.

"I'll never be a good school wombat, Mouse," he said sadly.

Mouse gave his paw a hug.

"Everyone can't be smart, Wombat!"

Tedda said: "Ark-ark!" as though he agreed, and Mouse made a very small ladylike face at him.

"If you cheer up, Wombat dear," it said, "you can enter a race! We're running races up and down the clearing. You can enter the race for animals under four."

"Under four what?" asked Wombat.

Mouse explained.

"I don't mind a bit if you don't enter the race, Wombat," said Tabby anxiously. "You just sit here and be miserable if you want to."

"You just want to win that race yourself, you Tabby Cat you!" squeaked Mouse.

Tabby preened himself. "Well, I don't see why your speedy pussy shouldn't, Mouse. I'm certainly faster than a koala, I hope, and *much* speedier than that baby ant-eater."

"But you're not faster than a wombat!" said Mouse.

109

"Course you aren't. You're not even as fast as Tedda!" said Wombat, suddenly taking interest. Tabby gave a squall of rage.

"I could beat that baldheaded old barker with my feet tied up!" he boasted.

"I'll *tie* your feet up if you call my Tedda names!" roared Wombat, and he forgot about being unhappy and chased Tabby down the clearing. In a moment they had reached the starting line, and just as Miss Roo cried "GO!" they shot across the line amongst the koalas and the other animals. In a second Tabby was out in front, his ears flat and his whiskers blowing in the breeze. He had a feeling that Wombat might very well sit on him if he caught him.

"Oh, everything happens to me!" he wailed, running for his life.

Now amongst all those young animals, Wombat and Tabby were the fastest except for one young grey rabbit. The little rabbit would have won the race if Wombat's hat hadn't blown off and pinned it to the ground. The hat wobbled along for a few yards, and then stamped off the track in a temper. And Wombat, with Tedda stuck in the front of his cardigan, trundled after Tabby.

"I'm going to tie your feet to your *ears!*" he promised. Tabby shrieked and flew to the end of the clearing. He was going to climb a tree and stay up there until Miss Roo came to protect him. But Wombat was so close behind him that they came to the finishing line together. Goodness knows who would have won if Tedda hadn't shot out of Wombat's cardigan and rocketed over the finishing line.

"Hooray!" cheered all the animals. "Tedda won!"

Wombat and Tabby forgot their quarrel. Tabby caterwauled with fury.

"That's not fair! That Tedda didn't even run!"

"That shows how fast he is!" said Wombat, sadly. "He didn't have to run in order to win. He's a much betterer racer than you or me, Tabby."

Now the prize for the race was a blue ribbon with a rosette. Tabby had wanted it very much, because he had thought it would make him look more handsome than ever. As Miss Roo tied it around Tedda's scraggy little neck, Wombat thought that he would have liked it, too. He could have given it to Mouse to make itself a new dressing-gown.

"That Tedda doesn't like me a bit," he said to Tabby.

"It's because he barks," explained Tabby. "He thinks he's a dog. That's why he ought to live with a dog."

"I do think you're right, Tabby dear," said Mouse.

Wombat thought it over. The black dog hadn't been at all rough with Tedda. He had just played with him. And, very likely, when Tedda barked, the dog had understood him perfectly.

"Aw right," he said. "You can go and live with the dog, Tedda."

Tedda broke into a great hoarse bark which went on and on and on, mostly because Tabby was poking his tummy. Wombat thought it meant that Tedda was glad.

After that Wombat really enjoyed the school picnic. He ran some more races, and he won the one for Hopping Animals in which he had entered by mistake. Tabby won the Climbing Relay with his team of three possums, and Mouse won a special prize as the Only Animal with Glasses. Wombat had five afternoon teas, and Tabby fell in the creek and caught a yabby accidentally. Luckily Miss Roo had brought some medicine which very quickly made his toes feel better.

Now the sun was low in the sky, and Miss Roo said that it was time to go. She blew a whistle to make all the pupils collect around her.

"First of all, pick up all the papers and scraps. Mouse, you're in charge!"

"Come along, all you bandicoots!" ordered Mouse. "Must leave the bush tidy!"

While Mouse was bustling around picking up litter, Tabby crept into the empty lunch basket and put the tea-towel over his head. He felt it would be a nice, restful change to be carried home by Wombat.

"Hurry up, Mouse, hurry up, Wombat!" called Miss Roo.

"Got to shake the crumbs out of our basket first!" called Wombat, busily trundling to the creek and shaking Tabby into the water. He *was* surprised to see the splash.

"I never met such a cat for swimming as you, Tab!" he remarked.

Tabby wanted to think of some splendid replies that would make even a muddle-headed Wombat mend his ways, but the water was too cold. Also, just then Miss Roo blew her whistle again. Tabby crept out of the water, shook himself, whispering piteously: "Everyone's mean to me!"

They hopped and scampered down the bush track. Now all the grass was in shadow and the tops of the gum trees red as fire with the sun.

"Hurry up, hurry up!" said Miss Roo. "We don't want to get lost in the bush!"

Wombat was at the end of the line. Something was making him feel strange and it wasn't the five afternoon teas. He waddled along for a while, absentmindedly woofling under the wet, steamy fallen leaves in search of beetles, and trying to make believe that he felt all right.

"Have I lost Tedda, have I, eh? No, he's down the front of my cardigan keeping warm. Then am I sorry for dropping Tabby Cat in the creek? No, because he's so terribubbly fond of swimming. And I haven't lost my Mouse because there it is, talking to Teacher. I know what the matter is," he said to Tedda excitedly. "We're going the wrong way."

"Ark!" remarked Tedda, which was not helpful.

Wombat wasn't sure if he should tell Miss Roo. He didn't want to worry her. But he didn't have to tell her.

Suddenly they came upon the creek again.

"Oh, look, everyone," cried Tabby importantly. "That's where I fell in. But I didn't complain a bit, even though I was wet and cold and nearly drowned. Brave cats like me don't complain."

"But the place you fell in was away up the track, Tabby dear," said Mouse. "It couldn't be here."

Tabby pointed out some pawmarks.

"There you are, Mouse. Who has pretty little feet like that? Only your brave pussy, that's all."

Miss Roo was looking upset.

"Goodness!" she said. "We've gone around in a circle. We're lost!"

CHAPTER V

Wombats are Waterproof

MOUSE thought they couldn't really be lost.

"I'm sure you go that way," it said briskly, waving a paw at the last of the sunlight.

"No, you don't, Mouse, treely ruly," said Wombat. But no one listened. They all followed Mouse down the track and around the rocks and in no time at all there they were back at the creek.

"Oh, look, everyone!" called Tabby excitedly. "There are my dear little pawmarks again."

"You just be quiet, you old cat!" snapped Mouse, who was looking very pink-nosed and disappointed with itself.

"*I'll* show you the way home," boasted Tabby. "Just follow your handsome little friend."

He bounded off into the scrub and the animals followed. Wombat didn't. He just waited beside the creek and thoughtfully ate a snail. And sure enough, in five minutes all his friends were back again.

"Hello," said Wombat.

"That's right," snarled Tabby. "Make fun of me! Perhaps I *can't* find the way home, but even a clever cat can't do everything. Why are you looking like that, Mouse?"

"A drop of rain just fell on my nose," quavered Mouse. Its pink nose was pale. "Oh, my, now we'll never get home."

Just then it started to rain very hard. The last of the light dwindled away and the bush filled with lonely shadows. The animals shivered and shook. Some of the smaller ones were frightened of the dark and began to cry. Miss Roo shooed them under bushes and told them to up-end the picnic baskets over their heads.

"What a very good idea," chattered Tabby. He whizzed in under the basket. Upturned, and standing on its handle, it looked like an interesting little house. There was room under there for two or three other small animals, too.

"I don't mind a rabbit, and I don't mind a bandicoot, but please," pleaded Tabby, "don't make me invite that soggy little anteater!"

But the anteater was already wearing his plastic lunch bag for an overcoat, and was very comfortable, with his long nose sticking out one corner.

"You may have my dear old hat for an umbrella, Miss Roo," said Wombat. "I don't need it. Wombats are waterproof."

They waited for a long time, but the rain did not go away. Now Big Bush was black as midnight, black as tar.

"Oh, dear," whispered Miss Roo. "Won't all the mothers and fathers be worried!"

"Don't cry, Teacher," said Wombat.

Miss Roo was surprised. "How do you know I'm crying?"

"Because I can see. Now you're taking out your hanky and now you're wiping your eyes. I know because wombats can see in the dark," explained Wombat.

Mouse felt around in the darkness until it touched Miss Roo's furry foot.

"Oh, Miss Roo, Wombat could lead us home. Couldn't you, Wombat dear?"

" 'Course I could," said Wombat excitedly, for he had so longed to show them the right way home, but no one had listened before.

He trundled out to the front. He picked up Mouse, wrung it out gently, for it was a sopping wet Mouse, and put it carefully in his cardigan pocket. Mouse snuggled down.

"You tell everyone what to do, Teacher, because you're so good at that," beamed Wombat.

So Miss Roo told her pupils to form a line, with the smallest in front. She was to be at the end of the line in case anyone was left behind.

"Every pupil hold firmly to the tail of the person in front," she said.

Tabby groped around in the darkness.

"I can't find a tail," he complained. "I'm being cheated. Who's that in front of me hiding his tail and being mean? And whoever's pulling *my* tail, stop it this minute!"

"Now, which way is home, Wombat?" asked Mouse.

"That way!" said Wombat. Mouse couldn't see which way he had pointed, but it felt sure he was right.

He was, too. In his mind's eye he could see his and Mouse's and Tabby's house amongst its dripping wet garden. All the windows were lighted and the red curtains shone warmly like red lamps. He could even imagine what they were going to have for supper—gingerbread! He gave a great joyful cackle.

"Come on, everyone!" he roared.

The track was muddy and slippery but luckily paws are safer than shoes for walking.

Miss Roo, like Mouse, felt sure that Wombat knew where he was going. She hopped along contentedly, being careful not to tread on any of her smaller pupils.

Halfway down the track, Mouse suddenly waggled its damp pink ears. It had heard something unusual. It stuck its head over the edge of the pocket and anxiously listened. It heard the plip-plop of large drops falling from leaf to leaf. It heard the swift little trickles of water on the stones. It heard someone in the bush calling: "Help! Help!"

"Oh, Teacher!" cried Mouse. "Someone has been left behind!"

Miss Roo called the roll. Everyone answered except Tabby. He had been trotting along, still with the basket over him, and without knowing it had left the line and gone off alone into the darkness.

"That naughty cat was told to hold the tail of the person in front!" squeaked Mouse.

But the person in front was shown to be a koala, which explained why Tabby couldn't find a tail.

"Funny old Tab," said Wombat. "I expect he's gone for another swim."

"Why, is the creek over that way, Wombat?" asked Miss Roo, very worried.

The next moment they knew it was, for there was a mighty splash and a caterwaul from Tabby.

"Told you," said Wombat proudly.

Tabby had trotted down a little hillside with the basket over his head, unable to see a thing, and had fallen into the creek just where it flowed fastest. However, he quickly bobbed to the top and climbed into the basket, which had jammed against a stone.

"Help! Help!" squawked Tabby. "Be quick!"

The basket was not made to be a boat. The water seeped in through the sides and bubbled through the corners. To make things worse the basket freed itself from the stone and bumbled off down the creek. The water pelted past, and the basket spun and rocked. Tabby clung to the handle, miaowing with fury and terror.

"I'm soaked right through the skin, right through to *me*! Doesn't anyone care?"

Just as Wombat got to the creek he saw the basket wobble around the bend and heard Tabby's fading cries.

"I know, Mouse," he said. "I'll pick him up at the bottom of the hill, after he goes over the waterfall. Won't that be excitabubble for him?"

Mouse felt that perhaps it wouldn't be, but it knew that Tabby could swim well and would be all right. Mouse thought they'd better get back to the rest of the animals.

There was a sigh of wind, and the rain spattered away over the treetops. Once it had stopped, the little animals found it easier to go down the track. Here and there in sheltered spots amongst the dry leaves, and in the doorways of little tunnels in the earth tiny greenish lights began to shine. They were dim, they were almost not there at all, but they were real lights.

"Glowworms!" cried Miss Roo. "Everyone pick one up!"

Soon you might have seen a procession of little green lights winking down the hill, for each little animal was carrying one very carefully in its paw. Things were much more cheerful then, and the possums began to squawk out a song.

"I do hope dear Tabby is all right," fussed Mouse.

Meanwhile Tabby had rushed down the stream like a rocket. Sometimes he was in the basket and sometimes he wasn't, clinging to the handle for dear life and bubbling and wailing and then going under once more. Then he heard the roar of the little waterfall. Tabby crouched in the basket and put his paws over his ears.

"I always said everything happened to me!" he moaned.

The roar grew louder. It was like fifty bathroom taps running at once. All at once the front of the basket tilted, and down went Tabby over the waterfall. Bubbles filled the air, waterdrops flew every way, and the basket spun down the waterfall and plopped into the pool. It quietly rocked over to the edge. Tabby opened his eyes.

"I'm safe! And I can see!" he whispered. For the moon had come up since the rainclouds had blown away.

"Oh, I'm a hero!" said Tabby, beginning already to feel better, but not much, for he was so wet and cold.

As the moonlight grew brighter and brighter, the glow-worms became dimmer and dimmer. The school pupils put them gently back into cracks in the rocks and holes in the banks, where they began to shine once more, for it was darker in those places. Now everyone could see treetops and shining wet leaves, and even the glisten of the creek at the bottom of the hill. They heard a wet cat complaining to himself.

"Why couldn't Wombat fall into a creek if a creek has to be fallen into? Why does it have to be me? If anyone has to get frozen and muddy and go over waterfalls, it's sure to be me. Nobody loves me, that's why."

"I do, Tab!" shouted Wombat.

Even shortsighted Mouse could see the shivering little shape of Tabby sitting up in his basket, which had been washed very handily onto the bank of the creek. He was the wettest cat in the world. His whiskers were plastered across the top of his head, and his fur was all licked backwards by the water.

When his classmates saw that Tabby was safe, they gave a tremendous cheer. Tabby recovered wonderfully, and bowed graciously.

"Oh, Tabby," said kind Miss Roo. "I *am* happy!"

"We're all happy," said little Mouse. "Because just look, we're home!"

And there across the creek was the edge of Big Bush. Wombat carried all the animals across in the picnic basket, and Miss Roo cleared the creek in one big hop. Everyone knew his way home from there. Soon each one was in his own home, getting his fur dried and eating his supper. Sometimes the supper was nuts and roots and fern sprouts, and sometimes it was grass or gumleaves or snails or worms, but that's the way supper is in Big Bush.

Mouse cooked the gingerbread and Wombat helped. Tabby, who had had so many awful adventures for a delicate cat, had a hot bath with Mouse's birthday bath salts in the water. Although they didn't smell like salmon, his favourite perfume, they did smell very good, like violets.

"And a cat likes to smell like violets sometimes," said Tabby to himself contentedly.

He dried his fur well with a warm towel and brushed it smooth again. He put on his smart, striped dressing-gown. Now he felt fine.

"I do believe I had a good day after all! How brave of me to feel like that, after all I went through! And now for some gingerbread, and some nourishing warm milk with a spot of codliver oil in it!"

Wombat was sitting at the table pretending to help Tedda chew a bone.

"He has to get used to living with a dog, dear old Tedda," he said. But now he didn't seem sad.

Mouse ate his gingerbread quietly and looked around the kitchen. All was cosy and bright and warm. Wombat's hat was hanging up to dry near the stove. Tedda looked happy to be going to live with the black dog. Tabby was bright-eyed and all ready to tell his friends about his frightful adventure with the waterfall.

"Oh, I am a lucky Mouse!" sighed Mouse.

Wombat knew what it meant.

"It's so comfortabubble to be us, isn't it, Mouse, eh?" he said.

The
Muddle-headed Wombat
on Holiday

CHAPTER I

The Birthday Surprise

THIS is about the day Tabby Cat decided it was time for Wombat's birthday. Tabby was smart, and so was his friend the pouched mouse, but Wombat was muddle-headed. He didn't even know when his birthday was.

"It seems such a little while since the last one, Tabby dear," said Mouse. "Don't you remember how he stepped in his birthday cake? He was picking hundreds and thousands out of his toes for weeks."

"No," said Tabby, "I've counted up on my paws, and next Saturday will be his birthday. You arrange the party, Mouse, and your handsome pussy will fix up a surprise."

Off he went to the garden shed and locked the door behind him.

Mouse was very excited. It shone up its small spectacles, put them back on its long, pink nose, and scuttled off to find Wombat, who was its best friend. Wombat was sitting in the yellow sunshine, eating a snail and being happy. He *was* surprised to find he was going to have a birthday.

"Will next Saturday be the eleventy-fifth of Remember, Mouse? Because *that's* my birthday."

"It could be," said sensible Mouse. "Who can tell?"

All at once they heard the sounds of hammering and sawing from the garden shed.

"How horribubbly exciting!" cried Wombat. "Tabby's making something. Let's go and look."

"No, it's a secret," explained Mouse.

"A secret from me!" grumbled Wombat, who felt that friends should never have secrets from each other. He trundled over to the shed door and gave it a kick. Then he banged it with his head. That hurt, so he became very cross.

"Open the door!" he roared.

"I won't!" squawked Tabby angrily. "Mind your own business!"

"Tell him to open the door and let me see, Mouse!" said Wombat.

"No, I won't," said Mouse calmly. "You behave."

Wombat trundled off grumpily. His feelings were hurt, so he pulled his raggy old straw hat down over his nose. He went and sat in Big Bush. The wind was blowing and the bush smelled of dead leaves and green leaves. Blue day-moths played in the grass. A frog made grating noises at the muddy edge of the creek. Soon Wombat became happy.

Meanwhile Mouse tapped at the door of the shed. Tabby wouldn't let it in. Mouse was so curious to know what Tabby's

surprise was that it forgot it was a well-brought-up mouse. It kicked the door.

"Mean old cat!" cried Mouse, holding its foot.

"If you're going to talk to your poor, dear pussy like that, I won't tell you *what* the surprise is," said Tabby, and he began to hammer very fast indeed, so that Mouse couldn't get a squeak in endways. So it went off and sat with Wombat and after a while it, too, felt happy again.

"You see, Wombat, Tabby is working on a surprise and it's for your birthday, and if you found out about it now, it wouldn't be a surprise."

Even a muddle-headed Wombat could understand that. He was so pleased he stood on his head, waved his stout legs in the air, and made great noises of joy and excitement. Oh, how he loved birthdays and how he loved his kind Tabby Cat!

Of course, really, Tabby was longing to tell Mouse all about the surprise and when Mouse said it was sorry for kicking the door he forgave it so quickly Mouse didn't have time to finish what it was saying. Then they crept off to the shed.

And, what do you think, Tabby Cat was making Wombat a caravan. There wasn't much of it to be seen, just some boards and nails and lots of sawdust.

"Tabby," said Mouse, "you're wonderful."

"I know," said Tabby. "Well now, Mouse, this is going to be a square, fat caravan, suitable for a Wombat."

"With wheels?" said Mouse.

"Of course there'll be wheels. One on each corner. They'll be yellow and black, and you may help paint them."

Mouse's nose turned pink as a sea-shell with excitement. Mouse loved to paint. But it had a question.

"How will the caravan move, Tab? Will you push it?"

Tabby could hardly believe his ears. "Who, me? A delicate little cat like me? Of course not, silly Mouse. We will tie it to Wombat's bike, and then he'll pedal away and off we'll go."

Mouse thought Tabby was very clever. Tabby quickly

banged some timber together into a box shape. He turned it over.

"Now, Mouse, be quiet. No little words of advice or anything like that."

Mouse said it wouldn't squeak a word.

Tabby fastened on the axle where the wheels would go. He slipped on the shiny metal wheels. He looked at Mouse. Mouse didn't say anything. Tabby gave a great caterwaul.

"You might have said something when I did it so beautifully. You could have said 'Well Done, Faithful Tabby,' or something like that."

So Mouse said it. It sighed, for it was very hard for a Mouse to know when to be quiet and when not. Suddenly it gave a little squeak of dismay. Looking through a small crack in the shed floor was a bright, brown eye. Mouse twitched its whiskers meaningly at Tabby. Tabby looked grim. They went outside the shed and around the side wall. Sticking out from under the shed was the end of a wombat. The shed was not very far off the ground, and Wombat was squashed flat on the

earth like a rather plump doormat, with his back legs sticking straight out behind him.

"Some animals," said Mouse sternly, "are not to be trusted."

Tabby gave a loud sob. "My surprise is spoiled," he moaned. "Oh, nobody loves me, everything goes wrong!"

Wombat was very ashamed when he heard Tabby crying. He wriggled out and pulled his hat down bashfully over his eyes.

"Wombat!" said Mouse. "You wicked, wicked animal, what did you see?"

"I saw Tabby hammering away at a dear little something. Mouse, is that my present?"

Then Tabby stopped crying. He saw that Wombat really didn't know what he was making. It would be a surprise after all. Wombat promised not to peek any more. And he didn't.

Tabby finished building the caravan and Mouse painted the wheels yellow and black like a bee's waistcoat, and sewed little white curtains for the window. It was the most beautiful caravan anyone could wish for.

When he saw it at last, Wombat couldn't believe his eyes. He looked at the door-knob, the front step, the curtains, the bunk, and the cupboards that opened and shut. He looked at the big hook which would fasten on behind his bicycle.

"It's not for me? Not treely ruly?"

"Yes, you may ride in it, and sleep in the bunk, and do anything you like with it because it's yours," said Tabby.

"You are the best cat in the whole world even if you *are* skinny and miserabubble-looking," said Wombat, and he gave

Tabby Cat such a hug that Tabby took ten minutes to untangle himself. By then Wombat was busily digging in the garden.

"What is he looking for?" said Mouse. "Worms, I believe. Imagine feeling hungry when he's just been given this lovely little caravan."

In a moment Wombat came in with his hat full of worms and snails. He began to put them in the caravan cupboard. Tabby turned pale grey with shock.

"He's putting those awful snails in the cupboard! Mouse, stop him!"

"I've never had any place to put my snails," said Wombat happily, "and now I've got a cupboard! Oh, thank you, thank you, Tabby."

Tabby lay down and cried quietly to himself. To think he had spent so much time working on that dear little cupboard and now it was full to the brim with snails! But Mouse sat on Tabby's chest and stroked his whiskers.

"Wombat's just being a wombat, that's all, Tabby dear. He thinks it's the best birthday present in the world! Just look at him, Tabby!"

So Tabby looked. The caravan was shaking all over as Wombat bounced with joy. The end of his silly scrap of a tail was sticking out the door and waggling with excitement. All sorts of happy wombatty noises came out of that caravan.

"He has to like things in a wombatty way, I suppose," said Tabby. "It's not as though he were sensible, like a cat or a mouse."

Just then Wombat backed out of the caravan.

"Now, I'm all ready. Who's coming?"

"Coming where?" asked Tabby, wiping away his tears with the end of his tail.

"For a pickwick! In my caravan!"

Tabby and Mouse were delighted. They loved picnics. Quickly they packed a lunch, sardines for Tabby and some

mosquito sandwiches for Mouse. They took fishing lines and bathing suits and woolly jumpers in case a cold wind blew. Mouse took its knitting. It was making some woolly gloves for itself, for next winter. And the more they prepared for the picnic, the more it seemed like a pickwick, which is a wombat word for a wombatty picnic, likely to turn out full of muddles.

Very soon you might have seen Wombat pedalling off on the bike with red wheels, with the lovely caravan bumping along behind. Mouse and Tabby were inside the caravan, and they didn't enjoy their ride a bit. They were very pleased when before them they saw the sea, blue as a bluebag, with white waves riding, and fish jumping for joy into the sunshine.

The caravan stopped. Tabby crawled out and lay on the sand.

"Oh, what a bumpy ride. Poor little delicate pussy, no one thinks that I might faint!"

Then he whuffled at the air.

"Fish! My favourite fruit!"

He felt much better after that.

Tabby and Wombat picked out a nice flat, rocky reef to sit on. They baited their lines. As for Mouse, it brought out a small muddly piece of green knitting and said it would sit in the sun and do some useful work.

So the pickwick started.

CHAPTER II

The Wonderful Caravan

WOMBAT and Mouse and Tabby Cat went for a pick-wick in the caravan which Tabby built for Wombat's birthday. Tabby and Wombat sat on a little reef and fished and fished. But no fish twitched at Tabby's line. Wombat didn't have any bites, either. But he was happy to sit in the sun and dream wombat dreams. As for Mouse, it got on with its knitting.

Suddenly Tabby, who so loved fish, and so longed to catch one, could bear it no longer. He gave a cry of sorrow. He said that everything happened to him and no one loved him, and what was the use of his going on a picnic when he couldn't catch a fish, and Wombat couldn't catch a fish either. Mouse, who was brave, and didn't approve of cats complaining, looked steadily through its tiny spectacles at Tabby, and when he stopped to take a breath it said calmly:

"I don't know about *fish*, Tabby dear, but there's a thing crawling up the rock near Wombat's paw."

Wombat and Tabby looked. There was a something with many legs or arms crawling like a spider up the reef. Mouse sensibly climbed to the top of a higher rock. Tabby's eyes

glistened. His mouth watered. His whiskers very nearly twanged with excitement.

"Oh, Wombat, a squid!"

"Is *that* what it is?" asked Wombat, very interested. "Well, all I can say is, squibs have very muddled-up faces. Worse than wombats, treely ruly."

"Catch it, catch it quickly!" screeched Tabby. "Squids are delicious. And there's such a *lot* of it."

Wombat was shocked. He saw that the little squid had eight short arms and two long ones, and that it was shy. It kept most of itself in the water. To think that Tabby would think of eating this nice creature with the muddled face!

"You're a cannibubble, Tabby!" he growled and he unhooked the squid's two long arms and tumbled it back into the water. It swam off in a very interesting way, like a little rocket ship. But Tabby danced up and down in rage and disappointment.

"Look what he did, Mouse! Just look! Threw six dinners and four lunches back into the water, all at once! Oh, how cruel!"

"I wouldn't let you eat that dear little squib, Tabby," said Wombat. "You just catch a fish!"

Tabby grumbled. He was trying his best already. He used all kinds of bait. He sat as still as a stone cat. But somehow the fish just wouldn't bite. He became more and more hungry. Wombat went to sleep in the sun, so it didn't matter about him.

As for Mouse, it knitted another finger on the very tiny mouse glove it was making. Sometimes it looked over the edge of the rock into the clear sunny water. It saw seven little fish, bright and swift as sunbeams, winking in and out the seaweed.

"Oh, there are some fish! I wish I could catch them for you, Tabby dear."

"Now, Mouse," said Tabby. "You know you haven't a line. You just attend to your knitting."

But it takes a great deal to stop a fat-tailed pouched mouse when that mouse has made up its mind. Mouse waited till Tabby was looking the other way. Then it lowered the little green glove, on the end of the long strand of green wool, into

the water. A fish snapped at the glove, and in a twink Mouse had it out on the rock.

"Oh, Tabby dear," said Mouse meekly. "Excuse me, but I've caught a fish with my knitting."

Tabby beat his paws on the rock. It didn't seem fair that he should fish for so long, with a real line and proper bait, and not get a nibble, and yet Mouse should catch a fish on the end of its knitting. Although the fish was only three inches long, Mouse staggered over to Tabby with it and put it on his lap.

"I caught it for *you*, Tabby dear! And I know you'll eat it, just for me."

So Tabby bristled his whiskers with joy, forgot his hurt feelings, and ate up every scrap of that fish. Meantime Wombat had awakened. He and Mouse stood proudly holding paws, while Tabby ate his fish.

"And now, you animals, darkness is coming, so we had better get our camp ready," said Mouse.

"Aren't we going to sleep in the caravan?" asked Tabby, choking a little over the last fin.

"We can't all fit inside," said Mouse. "One will have to sleep underneath. So I think we should draw straws."

It held out its pink paw. Three small straws stuck out.

Wombat and Mouse and Tabby each took one, and somehow Tabby got the shortest one.

"I have to sleep outside in the cold night, in the dark? All by myself? I'll be scared."

Mouse and Wombat didn't believe it.

"You're the bravest animal I know, Tab," said Wombat.

"And the handsomest." added Mouse.

"Why can't I sleep in the caravan?" wailed Tabby. "Suppose a wild animal comes in the night and eats me up?"

"Now, Tabby," said Mouse. "You're making a lot of fuss about nothing. Look how cosy it is under the caravan, just like a dear little house."

Certainly after Wombat and Mouse had hung some large leaves over the wheels to keep out the cold winds, and put down a blanket and pillow for Tabby to sleep on, the space under the caravan did look very cosy, like a nice cave.

"All the same, Mouse, I'll be alone and I'll be frightened! Aren't you sorry for your poor, nervous pussy?"

"If any large, wild animals come sniffing around, Tabby dear, you just call for me," said Mouse, and it trotted into the caravan and shut the door. It had a little matchbox bed in one corner, with its own pink quilt, and Wombat had the bunk, which was short and square and wombat-shaped. Soon Tabby heard big hearty snores from Wombat and fairy snores from Mouse. But he could not go to sleep. He heard mopokes, faraway and sad, calling in the bush. He heard the sea casting its white frills on the lonely sand in the moonlight. He saw big stars like pieces of ice.

"Everything happens to me," he moaned. "Why did I have to draw the wrong straw? Wombat and Mouse have warm beds in that dear little caravan, and here I am out in the dark. Oh, everyone's mean to me!"

But after a while he went to sleep. A long time afterwards he awakened in a great fright. Something was walking over his face. He gave a loud squall of terror, seized the something and stuffed it under his pillow. Wombat came trundling out of the caravan.

"What's the matter, Tabby? You'll wake up Mouse if you yowl like that."

"But a thing ran over my face. It had lots of legs and fur Oooh, I had such a fright, Wombat!"

"I expect it was a centipede. What a pity you didn't catch it. I love centipedes, they look *so* busy," said Wombat.

Tabby explained that the thing with fur and lots of legs was under his pillow right then. Wombat was delighted.

"Then don't let it get away, you clever cat. Perhaps I can make friends with it in the morning. And now let's go to sleep," said Wombat with a big yawn. He heaved himself down beside Tabby. Although Wombat took up a lot of room Tabby was very pleased. He snuggled up against his friend's broad brown back and went to sleep. Wombat had a happy thought about the nice little centipede he could make friends with in the morning, and then he, too, went to sleep. In the

morning Tabby awakened to see a bright red sky. It was daylight.

"Come on, wake up, wake up, Wombat."

"No, go back to sleep again," grunted Wombat. "Shall I tell you a bedtime story about spiders, dear little creepy, crawly things?"

Tabby gave a short squawk. He remembered that all night long a centipede had been under his pillow. He bounded out of bed.

"I'll just lift the end of the pillow very, very slowly, Wombat, and if it tries to get away, you grab it."

He lifted the pillow very carefully. Then he said in a small, meek voice, "Hello, Mouse."

A very squashed, ruffled Mouse stalked out.

"I've a good mind to bite you to the bone, you cat, you!"

"Are *you* the thing with dozens of legs that walked over my face in the night, Mouse?"

Wombat was very disappointed.

"It's not fair, Mouse. I thought you were a centipede and I like centipedes."

Mouse jumped up and down in rage. "I was worried about

Tabby and I came out to see how he was getting on, that's all."

"You didn't have to walk on my face," complained Tabby.

"How did I know which end your face was on, silly cat?" squawked Mouse. It really was in a fearful temper, because it's not at all comfortable to spend the night under someone's pillow.

"You animals don't deserve a mouse, that's all," stormed Mouse. "I've a good mind not to squeak to you for a whole day. And now I'm going to my own bed for a little sleep."

And Mouse tossed its long tail over its shoulder in a very haughty way and stalked into the caravan. Tabby and Wombat were very upset.

"How was *I* to know that it wasn't a centipede?" asked Tabby, piteously. "I don't see why Mouse is so cross with me."

"Never you mind," said kind-hearted Wombat. "Let's go back to bed and I'll tell you that lovely bedtime story about creepy, crawly spiders."

But Tabby didn't fancy it. He looked at the sea and thought of all the delicious breakfasts swimming about in it. He longed even more to catch a fish, or even eight fish.

"Suppose we went out in our rubber boat, Wombat! *Then* we might be able to catch some fish."

The rubber boat was really a beach float and could easily carry Wombat and Tabby and Mouse.

"But of course, Wombat dear," said Tabby, "you'll have to blow it up. A delicate little cat like me is no good for that sort of thing."

"That's all right," said Wombat. "I've got plenty of blow."

He took a big breath and then another one. He puffed up so much Tabby darted behind the caravan in case he exploded.

But he didn't. He used up all his air to blow up the beach float. It was a nice little boat, as red as a tomato. At once Tabby said he'd be captain and give the orders and Wombat could be the crew and do all the work.

Then Mouse came out of the caravan. It hadn't forgiven Tabby for mistaking it for a centipede and it was still rather cold and haughty. But it thought it might be fun to sit in the rubber boat and finish its knitting. So off they went. Wombat pushed the boat out, and jumped in quickly. Of course Tabby was already sitting in it. He said captains didn't get their paws wet. Mouse went quietly on with its knitting, keeping an eye on things just the same.

Do Wombats ever Bite Boats?

I T was such a shiny morning that Tabby began to feel lucky. Surely he would catch lots of fish today. His eyes turned green and dreamy and he imagined all the wonderful meals he would have. He would cook that fish in all sorts of delicious ways.

"Look, Tabby," said Mouse. "I've finished knitting one glove!"

"Fried!" said Tabby.

"Eh?" said Wombat.

"Boiled!" said Tabby. "And of course, steamed with butter.

151

So nourishing for a frail little pussy. I need building up, poor me."

They fished for a long time. The float tossed up and down as lightly as a leaf. The spray blew as clear as glass. The seabirds had pink legs and yellow legs and one tall grumpy one had cold blue legs. Mouse was so happy it went to sleep with its nose on its knitting. Wombat began to feel hungry.

"We forgot to bring any lunch, Tabby! And I didn't have my morning snail. I feel weak and wobbabubbly."

"Ssssssssh!" hissed Tabby.

"I wish I had a tomato," complained Wombat, "and an orange and some popcorn and some slugs and a big black beetle."

"I've got a bite! Will you be quiet, you awful animal?" squawked Tabby in a low, fierce whisper.

Wombat made a grumbling noise but he didn't say any more. He did want Tabby to catch a fish, but he was so hungry he didn't care very much. He looked longingly at the fat, bulgy red side of the rubber float and before he knew where he was he had taken a bite out of it. It didn't taste very good, rather like old sandshoe, but it was better than nothing, and he was grateful.

As for Tabby, he was having a very exciting time. He pulled hard on his line and up came the fish! It was enormous! Mouse woke up and cheered and clapped. Tabby wept tears of pride.

"Oh, I'm so happy! You must take a picture of wonderful me standing beside my wonderful fish!"

"Yes, but . . ." began Wombat. Mouse looked at him severely.

"I *do* think, Wombat dear, you might be more pleased when your second-best friend has caught such a tremendous fish . . . eeeyowwww, look at all the water in the bottom of the boat."

152

'Yes, we're sinking, Mouse,'' said Wombat sadly. "I was trying to tell you.''

Tabby pointed a shaking paw at the hole. He put the other paw over his eyes.

"Yes, wasn't I silly,'' said Wombat humbly. "I bit it!''

Mouse thought of a hundred things to say to Wombat, clever, useful things which a muddle-headed Wombat needed to have said to him after he'd bitten a hole in a boat. But there wasn't time.

"Someone must stick his head in the hole and stop the water coming in!'' ordered Mouse.

"I will, I will!'' cried Wombat, eagerly. "What fun!''

"No, your head is too big. Come along, Tabby.''

Tabby turned as pale as a grey cat can turn. He quavered: "Who, me?''

"Oh, Tabby, you could be a hero cat. Save us, dear Tabby!'' cried Mouse, scampering up Wombat's leg and on to his shoulder so as to get away from the water.

But it was too late. The boat was more than half full of water. In a moment it had gurgled down to the bottom and left Tabby and Wombat and the fish Tabby had caught, all

floating on the top. Mouse was sitting, quite dry and safe, in Wombat's hat.

"Somebody save my knitting!" cried Mouse.

"Somebody save my fish!"

But Wombat was too busy swimming for the shore, so Tabby had to rescue his fish for himself. Mouse waved comfortingly to him from a hole in Wombat's hat. It had saved its knitting and was very pleased about it.

"Don't be long, Tabby dear!"

"Oh, nobody loves me!" bubbled poor Tabby, as he bobbed along, towing his fish behind him.

He was so slow and sank so many times that at last he just held on to the fish as though it were a surf-board, and quietly coasted in to the beach. Wombat already had lit a fire of driftwood, and Mouse was poking twigs into it. The fire sparkled green and blue because there was salt on the wood.

"Poor dear Tabby," said Mouse kindly. "Bring him over to the fire, Wombat. No, Wombat, *not* by the tail, Wombat."

"It makes such a useful handle, Mouse," explained Wombat.

Tabby was very cold and wet and miserable. Mouse and Wombat took his mighty fish away and put it on the hot red

coals to bake. Wombat, who was very upset about Tabby, arranged him beside the fire so that his toes at once began to scorch, then trundled off importantly to have a word with Mouse.

"He might get a very bad cold, you know, Mouse. We should warm him up and rub his chest and horribubbly useful things like that."

Mouse thought they should, too. Wombat trundled importantly back to Tabby, who was beginning to feel better.

"You must be freezing, you nice ole Tab."

"Oh, I am, Wombat!" chattered Tabby.

"Would you like to come to the boil in the billy, Tab?"

Tabby stopped chattering at once. He scuttled around to the far side of the fire so that Wombat wouldn't get him. But Mouse was being important, too.

"You must do some exercises, Tabby dear. Just imagine if you caught a cold and spoiled your holiday!"

"Well, just for you, Mouse!" said Tabby unhappily. To his horror he found that Wombat was going to show him how. Wombat stood in front of Tabby and stretched up his paws. They didn't go very far because he is a fat wombat. Mouse gave the orders, because it is very good at giving orders.

"Ready, Tabby dear? One, two, three, *bend!* One, two, three, *bend!*"

Suddenly there was a sharp crack. Mouse was annoyed.

"Who is cracking?"

"It was my *neck!*" yowled Tabby. "I'm too delicate to do these horrid, rough exercises."

"Nonsense!" said Mouse sternly. "Now then, one, two, three, *jump!*"

Wombat was very willing. He wanted so much to show how well he could do the exercises. Still, he hadn't meant to jump on Tabby. He looked at Tabby's stretched-out form sorrowfully.

"Aw," said Wombat.

"Oh, he's all right," said Mouse. "I expect he's asleep. Well, let's go and slide on the sandhills till he wakes up."

Wombat made a glad noise. They hurried back to the caravan and found the bread-board. It was just right for

sliding. They slid down and climbed up until they were tired and very hungry, and then they went back to the fire.

Tabby had recovered from being jumped on, and was eating a good, hot, nourishing meal. Mouse gave a squeak of dismay.

"Leave some for us, Tabby!"

"You horribubble greedy old cat!"

"Delicious fish," gasped Tabby. "Tastiest fish I ever ate. Go away. I'm busy."

"But we're hungry, too!" roared Wombat. "Terribubbly hungry!"

"Go and eat snails, then," said Tabby, galloping around to the other side of the fish and beginning all over again. Mouse put on its sternest expression. Its spectacles shot sparks, small ones.

"Tabby, stop it at once."

"No, Mouse, it isn't good manners to leave any."

And Tabby didn't stop until he had eaten the whole of the big fish he had caught. Then he fell down and whuffed like a porpoise.

"Well, serve you right, Tabby Cat, I'm ashamed of you," said Mouse coldly. "I expect you'll be too sick to come for a

picnic tomorrow on the sandhills. I'm ashamed of you, Tabby Cat. You're a disgrace."

And Tabby *was* sick. He had a headache and a stomach-ache and a leg-ache and his paws felt funny. His whiskers hurt and his eyebrows hurt and all he wanted to do was to lie in the cool, dim caravan and not be bothered. In spite of its stern words, Mouse didn't want to leave him.

"Well, good-bye, Tabby. You look after yourself."

"Oh, who cares about me? I'm only poor, suffering Tabby."

Mouse patted him on the end of his nose and scampered off after Wombat. How sad Tabby was to see his dear friends going off for the day! First of all he had a miserable little weep. Then he decided to feel much sicker than he was.

"Oh, my tummy, my paws, my ears, eyes and nose! Oh, I'll die!"

But very soon Tabby stopped moaning because there's not much use in complaining when you're by yourself. He went

to sleep, which was very sensible. Very soon it was the middle of the day. Tabby awakened with a jump. He felt the caravan moving!

It was trundling slowly towards the sea. Tabby leaped from one window to another, but he could see nothing. He was tossed from side to side, he fell on his head, he fell on his back, he screeched and caterwauled. But no kind Wombat came to help. No brainy Mouse popped up to rescue him. Slowly the caravan squished to a stop.

"Oh, oh," moaned Tabby, "what an adventure for a refined little cat! It's too awful!"

He peeped out the window. There was water all around.

"Waves!" moaned Tabby.

Suddenly he thought he knew what had happened.

"Someone has run away with me. That's it, anyone would want to steal a valuable cat like me. I've been catnapped!"

Now, all this time Wombat and Mouse were having a wonderful time. Mouse was chasing Wombat along the beach,

and caught him every time, because Wombat fell over very often, on purpose. Then Wombat saw something exciting.

"Oooh, Mouse, there's another caravan, just like ours, only cleaner!"

He lifted up Mouse so it could look. Short-sighted Mouse squinted down the beach. It squeaked with astonishment.

"That's *our* caravan, silly! And it's in the water!"

"Well, why did Tabby push our caravan in the water, the mean ole cat?"

Mouse was worried. It didn't think Tabby had pushed the caravan into the water, because he was much too little.

"I do hope dear Tabby is all right," it said.

"So do I," said Wombat, "because I want to sit on him."

They hurried down to the water's edge. As soon as they

were near, they saw the anxious, grey face of their friend sticking out the window.

"Oh, you should have been here, you animiles," cried Tabby. "It was terrible!"

"Why did you push our caravan into the water, you mean ole cat?" grumbled Wombat.

"That's right, blame me," moaned Tabby. "I didn't push it at all. Someone catnapped me."

Mouse looked quietly around and saw that the caravan had run down the slope by itself. It was a great nuisance to have the caravan in the water. However, Mouse believed that nearly everything that happens can be fun if you look at it the right way.

"I'll tell you what, Tabby dear. Wombat and I will come in the caravan and then you won't be lonely and miserable any more. We'll pretend we're in Noah's Ark!"

"Tabby can be the elephant!" cried Wombat, delighted.

"No, I won't, I'll be the Tiger!" said Tabby crossly.

"I shall be the Mouse and hand around the lemonade," said Mouse calmly.

CHAPTER IV

Mr and Mrs Noah

WOMBAT carried Mouse across the water to the caravan. The little waves splashed about his knees. Wombat's knees are very near the ground, so you can see that the water wasn't deep. He climbed into the caravan and carefully shut the door. It *was* exciting to think they were going to play Noah's Ark.

By this time the sun was setting. A cold wind banged on the caravan window. Now that he had his friends with him, Tabby grew very brave and reckless.

"I think there's going to be a storm, but I don't care! It'll be fun!"

But Wombat was worried. "What about my bike if there's a storm? It might get frightened, out there in the dark!"

"Now, Wombat, don't make a fuss," began Mouse.

Wombat opened the door and fell out. There was a splash. Mouse shook its head sadly. It felt it might have known Wombat would fall in the sea. It peered through the blowy darkness. There was Wombat trundling up the hill towards his bike.

Luckily wombats are night animals and so he was able to see where he had left his bike. Puffing and chuckling he trundled down the hill again.

"I'm going to put you in the caravan, you poor little bike. I'll fit you in somehow even if I have to put Tabby Cat outside!"

There was a great commotion, rather like a small earthquake, with Wombat pushing the bike through the door and Tabby pushing it back and Mouse squeaking at them both.

Then Wombat and the bike fell backwards into the water,

which was now rather deep, because the tide was coming in.

"I hate cats, treely ruly!" roared Wombat.

"The bike won't fit, you silly muddle-head," remarked Mouse. "Just tie it to the caravan axle and come inside, there's a good wombat."

This was the most sensible thing to do, so, muttering and growling, Wombat did it. Then he lumbered into the caravan, streaming wet.

Tabby gave a shriek and jumped to the top of the cupboard.

"Don't come near me, you awful wet wombat!"

Suddenly Wombat forgot he felt bad-tempered. He beamed all around.

"Let's all have a snail!"

Tabby had a salmon sandwich and Mouse had a toasted mosquito, and then they all felt much better.

"When do we start playing Noah's Ark?" asked Wombat.

"Because I want to change. I want to be Mr Noah and Mouse can be Mrs Noah and . . ."

"Who am I?" cried Tabby indignantly.

"You can be all the animals," said Mouse smartly.

Tabby was delighted. It would be fun to be the tiger, but much better fun to be a tiger and a penguin and a snake and a hippopotamus all in one.

He climbed on top of the bunk and looked at the window. The water was black and angry, hissing around the caravan steps and doing its best to creep through the floor. But none came in, because Tabby had built the caravan very strongly. Tabby felt that the caravan was rocking from side to side.

"You don't suppose . . . ?" he whimpered.

"Oh, *no*," cried Mouse.

"We're floating, just like the real Ark!" cheered Wombat.

They were, too. Tabby jumped into the bread-tin and shut the lid. Mouse was frightened, but tried not to show it. Wombat just loved his new adventure.

"Are you feeling miserabubble, Mouse? Because your nose looks miserabubble. All pink."

"Never mind my nose!" snapped Mouse. "Of course I'm miserable. And you would be too, if you had any imagination."

"I've got a tomato sandwich instead," said Wombat, and he took a squashed sandwich out of his cardigan pocket and gave half to Mouse, beaming away as though he hadn't a care in the world. At the sight of his happy face, Mouse cheered up a little, blew its nose on a handkerchief as big as a postage stamp, and arranged its damp whiskers.

"You're quite right, Wombat, we must be brave."

Tabby popped up out of the bread-tin, covered in crumbs.

"All very well for you, Mouse. I don't want to be a Robinson Crucat. I'm not a big, brave mouse like you, you know. I'm just a poor, delicate little pussy."

Wombat pushed him down inside the tin and put on the lid. They could hear him fuming away inside.

Then Mouse and Wombat went to sleep. Mouse woke up very often in a worried way, but Wombat snored happily, kicking away now and then as though he were having exciting dreams. When the day came it was a grey, watery, weepy day indeed. Wombat climbed up, rubbed a clean spot on the window and put his buttony brown eye to it.

"No land anywhere! Never mind, let's play our Noah's Ark game. Come on out of the bread-tin, Tab."

Tabby rose up, glaring terribly, with a slice of bread on his head. Wombat snatched it off and ate it.

"We're going to play Noah's Ark, Tabby dear," said Mouse. "And remember, you're all the animals."

"Won't be all the animals," spat Tabby, who was very offended at being in the bread-tin all night.

"Oh, Tabby, please play," said poor Mouse. "It'll cheer us up. Please, dear, clever, handsome Tabby! After all there's

not another cat in all the world that could be all the animals in the Ark at the same time."

Tabby said that was true, and he bowed all round and sprang out of the tin. Very soon they were all playing Noah's Ark, and forgot their troubles. Mouse and Wombat thought they had been very clever coaxing conceited Tabby to do what they wanted. But Tabby came out best in the end.

"I expect Mrs Noah was a very busy lady," Mouse said. "Feeding all those animals! People get so hungry on board ship. It's the sea air."

"And all the animals are hungry right now," said Tabby. He gave a snarl. "Now I'm the tiger. That means I want a sausage for my breakfast."

So Mrs Noah cooked a sausage for the tiger's breakfast. As soon as the sausage was eaten, the tiger became a seal.

"Fish! Fish!" barked Tabby.

So Tabby had a tin of sardines and enjoyed them very much. After that he became a horse and ate all the biscuits.

It was quite a relief to Mr and Mrs Noah when all the animals became seasick and lay down on the bunk and moaned.

"May I go fishing, Mouse, eh?" asked Wombat. "I could open the window and throw out the fishing line and catch some tins of sardines for poor sick Tabby."

Tabby gave a wail. He didn't want to hear about sardines, ever, ever again.

Mouse thought fishing was a good thing for Wombat to do. It would keep him busy and contented. A little while later you might have seen Wombat sitting beside the open window, holding the end of his line. The storm had blown away, and

the sky was blue and clean. Now and then a seagull flipped across the window like a scrap of white paper.

Mouse saw that there was no land to be seen, and sighed sadly. Wombat patted it lovingly on the head. After it had got up again, it said:

"I do try to be brave, Wombat."

"Well, I'm not brave," said Wombat. "I'm just muddle-headed and it's very comfortabubble. *You* try being muddle-headed, Mouse."

Suddenly Mouse forgot about being miserable, for Wombat's fishing line straightened out, as stiff as a poker, and the caravan leaped in the air. Tabby fell out of the bunk and awoke in a fright.

"What's happened? What's happened?"

"Wombat's hooked an enormous fish!" squeaked Mouse. "It's the biggest fish in the whole sea! Look, Tabby, look!"

Tabby saw the tail of the fish whip out of the water, shiny black. He was so excited to see so much fish that he forgot about being seasick and caught hold of the line with Wombat and began to pull and tug. But the big fish was so strong that

it pulled the caravan whizzing through the waves. The foam flew up on both sides as white as milk.

"We'll have our picture taken with the big fish!"

"Our names will be in all the papers!"

"Won't the bush animals be proud of us?"

"Hero Cat catches monster fish!" crowed Tabby. Wombat stuck his lip out.

"Hero Wombat catches monster fish, *too!*" he growled.

Just then the monster fish leaped in the air, spun on its tail and dashed past the caravan in a cloud of spray. The caravan jerked around and flew after the fish like a speedboat. And Tabby saw something in the distance! It was the beach!

"We're being towed back to land!" he shouted.

Very soon they could see the breakers. The fishing line twanged and snapped, and Wombat and Tabby fell in a heap

in the corner. At first they didn't know what had happened, and just lay there blaming each other and being very disagreeable.

A big wave rose softly, softly, under the little caravan and wafted it in to the beach. It dropped it on the sand as lightly as a bubble.

"Oh, my," breathed Mouse. "We're on land again."

"But where's our fish?" screamed Tabby. "It's gone, it's got away. And I was going to have my picture in the paper and be Hero Cat and everything."

He stepped up on Wombat's head and looked out the window. There was the sunny beach, and no fish at all.

Tabby sobbed with disappointment. But Mouse danced for joy, it was so glad to be back on land. After all, it was a land mouse and not a sea mouse. Wombat was delighted, too. He hurried out, stood on his head in the sand for a moment, then untied his bike and pedalled away with the caravan behind him. Soon they were amongst the warm sandhills, so Wombat stopped.

Tabby opened the caravan door and strolled out.

"Well!" he said. "What an adventure. Of course *I* wasn't scared. You animals are lucky you had me with you to cheer you up."

"You have a breadcrumb on your ear," said Mouse coldly. Tabby's ears and paws turned pink. He felt ashamed of his boasting. Mouse gave him a glare and climbed into its match-box bed.

"Whatever's the matter, Mouse, are you sick?" asked Wombat.

"No, I'm just tired. I'm tired of cats and wombats and pickwicks."

And Mouse pulled the pink quilt over its head and wouldn't squeak another word. Wombat and Tabby were very upset.

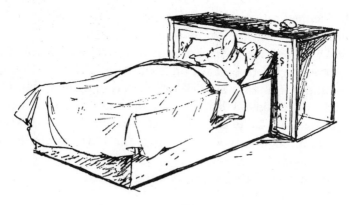

They went around the other side of the caravan and had a solemn important talk.

"I believe that poor little animal is worn out, Tab."

"We must look after our Mouse, Wombat!"

"We could make it hot drinks and put ice on its little head and be kind and useful!"

"We could play doctors!" said Tabby happily, for he loved playing doctors. So did Wombat.

Dr Tabby and Dr Wombat shook paws, then they began to plan how they would help Mouse recover from its pickwick.

177

CHAPTER V

Home is Best

MOUSE was very tired after all its adventures. It needed to have a quiet sleep. Wombat twitched the pink quilt off it, and Mouse twitched it back. Wombat twitched it off again. Mouse's nose turned rosy with rage.

"Perhaps you'd like a good nip on the paw, you muddle-head, you?" asked Mouse.

"I'm Doctor Wombat," beamed Wombat, "and I'm going to look after you."

"And I'm Doctor Tabby," explained Tabby pompously, "and I'm going to look after you too."

"Thank you very much," said Mouse, "but I'll be quite well after I've had a little sleep."

"Very good," said Doctor Tabby, "but first you must have

your wash. That's very important. When I was in hospital when I hurt my paw, the nurses kept washing me all the time."

Now fat-tailed pouched mice are the daintiest little animals in the bush. Mouse's feet were as pink as popcorn; its ears were like petals; its glasses glittered like drops of dew. Its toenails (if you could see them, for they were so small) were a credit to it. But here were Tabby and Wombat excitedly standing beside its bed, wanting to wash it.

"There's nice hot water in this basin, Mouse," said Wombat, "and I brought along the pot-cleaner and the sandsoap just in case."

"I won't, I won't," cried Mouse.

"Doctor Tabby knows best, Mouse dear," said Tabby.

"And Doctor Wombat knows second-best," added Wombat.

The next moment a hot soapy wash-cloth was walloped all over Mouse's face. Then Tabby screamed. Wombat shook his head sadly.

"Mouse, it isn't *nice* to bite doctors. I shall have tu wash your paws myself."

"I won't have my paws washed, I won't have my paws washed!" yelled Mouse. It kicked and bounced with rage. There was a crash. Tabby was shocked. As for Doctor Wombat, he spoke in a trembling voice:

"I was just trying to help because I love you so terribubbly and I want to look after you. And now I've got water all down

my cardigan, and my dear old hat is all wet and drippy, and . . ."

"Grrr!" said Mouse, and it pulled the quilt over its head and muttered away crossly to itself. It seemed to Mouse that a small animal who wanted a peaceful sleep couldn't find it anywhere. It was very sad.

Meanwhile Doctors Tabby Cat and Wombat sat dismally on the caravan step. They couldn't understand why Mouse

wanted to be left alone. It didn't seem to be what friendly little Mouse would want.

"Imagine kicking the water all over you, Wombat! Our Mouse!"

"Imaginabubble," agreed Wombat gloomily.

"But Doctor Tabby knows what the matter is, Wombat. Mouse has a temperature."

Wombat was interested. "May I have one too? I'm starved."

"It's when you get a hot head, Wombat. You feel all queer and different. We must get something cool to put on dear little

Mouse's dear little hot head, Wombat. Some ice or something."

Tabby knew there was a little beach shop over the sandhills and on the main road. It would be quick and easy for Wombat to pedal off on his bike and fetch some ice. Wombat was delighted. He very much wanted to help.

"I'll be so fast, treely ruly, Tab! You just see!"

"And hurry, Wombat, or the ice will melt!"

Wombat rushed off. He didn't want his Mouse to have a hot head and be cross with him. He pedalled so fast his short legs were a brown blur. Soon he came to the little beach shop. He panted inside. The lady *was* pleased to see him, and he was pleased to see her. They beamed at each other for a while, then Wombat stuck his lip out.

"I forgot what I came for."

"Bread, butter, jam, sugar?" asked the lady, who was helpful.

A great lump stuck in Wombat's throat. To think that his dear Mouse was sick and grumpy and he couldn't remember what it needed to make it better. Then he rattled his head.

"I know. I want something cold!"

The lady said she had all kinds of ice cream, chocolate, vanilla, strawberry and lime. They all looked so pretty that Wombat couldn't decide. Then he thought that the strawberry ice cream might go nicely with Mouse's pink ears.

"That one!"

It was strawberry. Wombat felt very important. He remembered that Tabby, who knew so many things, had told him to hurry or the ice would melt. Where could he put it?

"In my dear old hat! *That's* a safe place!"

He quickly put the ice cream, which was in a small box, on top of his head and popped on his hat again. He was so pleased to be so thoughtful and clever that he pedalled back to the caravan at top speed.

Tabby met him, paw at lips.

"Quiet, Doctor Wombat, the patient is asleep. Where's the ice, you muddle-head?"

Wombat proudly took off his hat. The ice cream had melted a little. Small pink rivers had trickled down amongst Wombat's fur. Tabby gave a caterwaul of rage and disappointment.

"Ice cream! I said ice!"

"So you did," said Wombat, sorrowfully. Then he brightened up: "But it's terribubbly nice ice cream, Tab. Strawberry!"

"How can I put strawberry ice cream on Mouse's little hot head, you wombat, you?" moaned Tabby. He sobbed broken-heartedly. "Oh, why did I ever become your second-best friend? I'm not strong enough for wombats!"

Just then out strolled Mouse. It had had its sleep, and it was feeling its own cheerful self again. It was wearing a very sporty pair of white shorts and a shirt to match. First of all it saw Doctor Tabby lying on the ground sobbing and kicking with rage. Then it saw its Wombat, whiskers drooping, lip stuck out, standing there miserably with a packet of ice cream on his head. Mouse saw at once that a mouse's loving paw was needed.

"Oh, Wombat, you dear thoughtful animal! Ice cream, and my favourite flavour, too!"

"Eh?" gulped Tabby.

"Treely ruly, Mouse?"

"Just what a tired Mouse needs! Ice cream! Let's eat it before it melts," said Mouse, bustling around getting saucers and spoons for everyone. "Here's yours, Doctor Tabby."

"I don't think I'll be a doctor any more," said Tabby. "I'm too delicate."

"And here's yours, Wombat!" said Mouse. It hopped on Wombat's lap and ate its ice cream there, and because it was such a dainty Mouse it didn't drop a drip on its new white shorts. Tabby began to feel stronger, and Wombat's miserable whiskers straightened out and even began to curl up at one side.

"Oh, that was horribubbly delicious!" said Wombat as he spooned up the last of his ice cream.

"Rather like strawberry soup, but quite tasty," remarked Tabby.

"And now what shall we do?" asked Mouse.

Wombat felt that he had had enough pickwick, but he didn't like to say so. Tabby felt he had had enough pickwick,

but he thought that perhaps Mouse wanted some more adventures. So Mouse felt that it was the one to speak.

"I'm feeling homesick, you animals."

"Does that mean you have a wobbabubbly feeling in the tummy, and a sad feeling under the cardigan, and paws that

want to go *that* way?" asked Wombat, as he pointed towards Big Bush. Tabby and Mouse nodded eagerly.

"Then we shall go home!" chirruped Mouse.

This time Mouse sat on the handlebar and rang the bike bell. Tabby sat on top of the caravan and rocked and swayed and pretended he was a sailor on a sailing ship. They pedalled along the road, away from the sandhills and the sea. They saw

no more sea-birds, only a tall, white heron standing on one leg beside the lily lagoon.

"We're not far from Big Bush now!" squeaked Mouse. Oh, how happy it was!

The caravan hit a bump and the sailor shot off headfirst into a clump of swamp grass. Luckily it was soft and muddy and Tabby didn't hurt himself.

"Oh, everything happens to me! Wombat and Mouse don't even know I'm gone!" he wailed, as he watched the caravan bumping along behind the bike with red wheels. He saw that

the heron was looking at him with a round, yellow eye. Tabby arched up his back and smiled haughtily.

"Don't think I'm a frog! I'm a very refined cat, come upon hard times!"

But the heron stabbed at him with its long bill, and shrieking, Tabby rushed after the fast-disappearing caravan. He had a very awful time. He had to swim the lagoon, and like all cats he hates swimming. Then he met a water-snake, and climbed up on a lily leaf to get away from it. Of course the leaf sank, and Tabby not only became wetter and muddier than ever,

but was chased away from there by a furious mother frog who had never seen a cat before and didn't want to see one again.

Tabby limped into the warm shelter of Big Bush. There were all the trees he knew. There was the tall bluegum with Mrs Koala's little house on the top of it. Surely she'd be pleased to see him!

"Look, Mrs Koala, it's me, your little Tabby Cat!" he called. Mrs Koala, who was having her afternoon tea, at once threw a cake at him. She didn't usually throw cakes at people,

but she did not recognize the sleek, grey shape of Tabby under all the mud. It was a very hard cake, one of Mrs Koala's best, and Tabby staggered onwards, looking for his Mouse and his Wombat.

Meantime Mouse and Wombat, not knowing they had lost their friend, had come within sight of their house. It looked so cosy, with the sunset shining on its windows, and the garden grown high about the steps, that Mouse wiped away a happy tear with the end of its tail. The flowers were taller than Wombat, and the grass was taller than Mouse.

"We'll have to do lots of work, Wombat dear!"

"Yes, but think of all the scrumptious beetles we'll find!" said Wombat joyfully.

"Wait for me, wait for me!" said a sad voice, and down the track trotted a small, muddy figure.

"Why, Tabby dear! How did you get there? You should have been on the top of the caravan!" cried Mouse.

"I was bumped off," said Tabby haughtily, "by a certain person, who *will* ride over stones, even though his second-best friend is on top of the caravan."

"Never mind, we're all here now," chuckled Wombat, "and isn't it comfortabubble!"

And even though Tabby was wet and muddy and had been chased by herons and frogs and water-snakes and indeed was full of all the dreadful things that can happen to poor, delicate little pussies, he looked at the cosy little house and agreed.

"Pickwicks are fun!" he said.

"Pickwicks are horribubble fun! Treely ruly," said Wombat.

"But home is best," said little Mouse.

The Muddle-headed Wombat
in the Treetops

CHAPTER I

The Wonderful Idea

TABBY CAT was the second-best friend of the Muddle-headed Wombat and his Mouse. Tabby was a small grey cat with big ears and a skinny tail. Still, he thought he was very handsome, and often reminded his friends of his good looks. He also believed he was very delicate and needed to be looked after much better than he was.

Of course, living with a wombat does make a cat jumpy and sometimes Tabby thought he could not stand another day of it.

"See how my paws shake!" he said. "And I've lost my

appetite, you know. Last night I had two tins of sardines for supper, and I left *three tails*!"

"Perhaps you need a tonic, Tabby dear," said kind-hearted Mouse.

Wombat bounced up and down excitedly.

"I'll make it for you, nice ole Tab! I'll put dead leaves in it, and lovely mud!"

Tabby shrieked and fled up the big pine tree.

"Nobody loves me," he moaned. "It's just like that awful Wombat to put mud in his dear pussy's medicine."

Then, all at once, Tabby had a grand idea.

"I love Mouse and Wombat, but a frail little cat like me needs a place of his own. I'll build myself a house, and I'll build it in this tree. Mouse and Wombat won't be able to bother me, because they aren't climbing animals."

Tabby laughed so much he fell out of the tree. However, he didn't hurt himself, and lay on the grass chuckling and wriggling with joy. Wombat was worried about him. He couldn't think of any other way to help, so he sat on Tabby. Tabby went on laughing, though in a squashed way. He gave Wombat a hug.

"I'm going to build a treehouse!"

"Oh, Tabby!" breathed little Mouse.

Wombat's whiskers twanged. He didn't know what a tree-house was, but he could see it was something wonderful. He could see by the way Mouse's nose had turned pink.

"I shall have a red door, and a shiny knocker shaped like a fish, and a real stove on which I can make toast, and heat up nourishing little cups of cocoa."

Mouse could just see that little dolls' stove, twinkling bright, with mouse-sized saucepans and a frying-pan as big as a shilling.

"Oh, Tabby," it breathed, "I just can't wait to live there!"

Tabby put on a surprised face.

"But Mouse, this treehouse is just for me. It's a place for me to go when I'm feeling delicate."

Wombat gave a squawk.

"We're coming to live with you, Tab! Think how misera-bubble you'd be without us."

Tabby smiled smugly.

"Then *we'd* be miserabubble!" roared Wombat.

"But Wombat dear," purred Tabby. "You couldn't climb the tree. After all, wombats are digging animals. Your claws are no good for climbing trees. What a shame!"

"You're a mean old Tabby Cat," squeaked Mouse. "You just want to get away from us!"

It gave Tabby such a kick on the back leg. But it was a very small animal and Tabby did not even notice. Mouse's glasses misted over. It sobbed a fairy sob. But Tabby went on talking excitedly.

"Oh, to think that soon I'll be away from bothersome wombats and mice. How I'll enjoy sitting high amongst the branches and dropping pine cones on your old muddle-heads!"

"You can't have the pine tree!" said Wombat. "A mopoke lives there already."

"Oh, pooh!" said Tabby. "What's an old mopoke to a brave bold cat like me? Where's the hammer, where are the tacks?"

He bounded off to fetch these important things. Wombat and Mouse looked at each other dismally.

"I want to visit Tabby in his treehouse. I do, treely ruly," said Wombat in a trembling voice.

"But we aren't climbing animals, just as he says," pointed out Mouse.

"I know," said Wombat. "We'll saw the tree down!"

"But that might hurt darling Tabby."

"He's not darling Tabby. He's horribubble Tabby,"

growled Wombat. He cheered up a little. "Well, maybe that mopoke will get him."

Mouse was sensible. Mouse was thinking.

"We'll be good, useful animals, and then Tabby will see he can't do without us."

"And then he'll invite us to visit him, and he'll think of some way for us to climb the tree, and everything will be all right!"

Wombat lay down and kicked his stout legs with joy. Tabby tottered past with a load of timber. He stopped and looked at Wombat a little fearfully. What could he be so happy about? Tabby thought:

"I don't like it. That animal is planning some dreadful

trick to play on his handsome pussy. I must be very careful."

He climbed up the tree many times until he had lots of timber and tools stacked in a crotch of the tree. He had other things, too, sunburn cream, and cooling drinks, and a bucket of water for washing his paws. The mopoke who lived in the pine tree took fright and blundered out into the sunlight. Mouse dived into Wombat's cardigan pocket. No mouse trusts owls. The mopoke flopped into another tree and sat sulking. Tabby paid no attention. He began to build the platform upon which his treehouse would stand.

Presently his dear friends had thought of a way to be useful.

"He must be so hot and tired, Wombat. We'll make him a cup of tea!"

Wombat was happy. "That would be terribubbly helpful. Shall I boil the william?"

"Boil the billy, Wombat," explained Mouse. Wombat

wasn't listening. He was trundling around gathering twigs and cones.

"Let's boil the william under the pine tree, Mouse. It will be cosy for poor hard-working Tabby."

Mouse smiled a mischievous smile.

Soon Tabby began to cough. Smoke rose all around him. He could barely see his paw in front of his eyes.

"Look, Tabby," squeaked Mouse happily. "We're making you a helpful cup of tea. We're going to do this every day."

Tabby caterwauled with rage. "If you do, I'll be a smoked cat!"

"But still, you'll have a nice cup of tea," said Mouse.

The next moment, down swooshed the water Tabby had

taken up for washing his face and paws. The fire and Wombat and Mouse were all put out together. The friends crept off, talking loudly about ungrateful cats.

"Never mind," said Mouse, "let's think of something else."

But they couldn't. Wombat was muddle-headed, and so he couldn't, and brainy Mouse didn't feel brainy at all. This made them very cross. They went back to the tree and begged and threatened. Tabby took no notice. He just went on building. He had already made the platform and one wall. They seemed very neat and strong.

"I'm going to have a letterbox, too," he boasted.

"What letters will be delivered away up there, silly cat?" asked Mouse scornfully.

"Airletters, of course," replied Tabby haughtily.

That mopoke will come and peck you because you've taken his tree," said Wombat. "If you let us visit you, we'll chase him away for you. We're terribubbly good chasers, aren't we, Mouse, eh?"

"I'd rather have the mopoke, thank you," replied Tabby, as he dropped a pine cone on Wombat's head.

Mouse and Wombat had hurt feelings. Still, Mouse explained that it didn't help to get angry.

"If we could only get into the tree some way, Wombat dear, we could do useful things, like finding the tacks, or holding the hammer, or painting that little red door. But Tabby would never let us into the tree."

"Suppose we gave him a present," said Wombat. "He likes fish, you know, it's his favourite fruit. Suppose I hid in the dry leaves and made a noise like a sardine. He'd probabubbly come down to look, and then we could hurry up into the tree and there we'd be."

Mouse had never heard a sardine make a noise, but Wombat explained that was because they were usually shut up in tins.

"They make a noise like this," he said. He squinched his

202

face into a poky shape and made a noise like a cricket.

"Well, get the ladder, Wombat," said Mouse.

Wombat fetched the ladder and put it at one side of the tree where Tabby could not easily see it. Then he hid in the leaves and made a noise like a sardine. At once Tabby flickered out of the half-built treehouse.

"Mouse, Mouse, come and save me. There's a rat somewhere around this tree. I hate rats! Oh, I shall faint!"

Mouse looked more than usually brave. Wombat squeaked again.

"Oh, my, Tabby dear," said Mouse. "That wasn't a rat, that was very likely a sardine."

"I've never heard a sardine make a sound like that," said poor Tabby.

"That's because you're so busy eating them, I expect," explained Mouse. Tabby brightened.

"Perhaps you're right. So that's the noise they make, sweet little things."

Tabby did not need to be told to come down and look for the sardine. He was hungry after all his hard work and he

leaped out of the tree and began to search. Wombat scuttled out from under the leaves and began to climb the ladder. But wombats are not made to climb ladders, either. He had not gone very far before he fell through the rungs.

Tabby was furious.

"I might have known, you tricky pair of animals. Oh, you should be ashamed!"

Mouse and Wombat *were* ashamed. They stood with drooping ears and not a word to say. Tabby flew up the tree and began dropping cones like hailstones. Wombat was glad he was wearing his hat. Besides being good for many other things, it kept pine cones off, like a roof.

"No wonder Tabby doesn't want us in his little tree-house," said he sadly. "We're horribubble, Mouse."

"I feel so mean," said Mouse. "He was so disappointed about that sardine. Let's go and catch him a real fish."

"And we won't pester him about the treehouse any more," agreed Wombat. "We'll be as good as good."

In the little brown creek that whispered along at the end of the garden there were many small fish. Tabby often went there and tried to coax them to jump out, but they never did. Tabby was not clever at fishing, but Wombat was. He found his line and fishing bag and some bait and off they went. Mouse said it would sit beside him and tell him a story so that he wouldn't go to sleep. That was brave of Mouse, because Wombat was the worst interrupter in the world.

"This story is about a dog, Wombat," said Mouse. "Are you listening? Well, once upon a time there was a little dog."

"I know why he was little," said Wombat. "He wouldn't eat his vegetabubbles. No wonder he was little."

"He was little because he hadn't grown up yet," said Mouse hurriedly, "and his name was Jumpy."

"Why?" asked Wombat. "What made him jump? Did he ever stop? What about when he went to bed? Go on, tell me, Mouse. Go on. Eh?"

Just then Mouse saw Wombat's line dive to the bottom of the creek. It was glad because now they would have a fish for Tabby. It was also glad because now it wouldn't have to finish the story and keep explaining things all the time.

Wombat pulled out the fish. It was very big, and the friends knew that Tabby would be delighted. They could not rush off to the pine tree quickly enough.

Tabby was still very busy. He was sitting on the frame nailing the roof into place. When his friends hurried up, Tabby

gave them a grass-green glare. He lashed his tail to show he had not forgiven them.

"Oh, Tabby, Tabby, see what we caught for you!"

Tabby sneered. One set of his whiskers almost touched his eyebrow on that side.

"Aha, you think you can trick me again, don't you, just because I'm a trusting little pussy. Well, you can't, so there. Aha!"

"Don't you aha at my fish, you ole Tabby Cat," growled Wombat, very offended.

"I shall aha if I wish. Because that is not a real fish!"

"What do you mean?" cried Mouse.

"It's made of rubber, or plastic, *I* know," said Tabby, sneering again. This time his whiskers did meet his eyebrow and he had to untangle them quickly.

"But we caught it in the creek, Tabby dear," said Mouse tearfully. "For *you*, Tabby. Just to show we're sorry for playing that trick about the sardine."

"Aha!" said Tabby proudly, and he gave a nail a whack

and nailed some of his fur to the roof. That made him more angry than ever, and he would not listen to Wombat and Mouse any more.

Wombat took off his hat and cried a few tears into it. Mouse added some more—very small ones, like dewdrops.

Suppose Tabby never made friends with them again?

CHAPTER 11

Tea in the Treehouse

W OMBAT and Mouse sadly put their fish at the foot of the pine tree and went home. They had thought that Tabby would be so happy to have such a delicious present. As for Tabby, he sat outside his half-built treehouse and thought how clever he'd been.

"They can't pull the fur over my eyes! Imagine trying to trick their second-best friend with a plastic fish!"

But somehow being clever didn't stop Tabby from being lonely. Though he loved his house in the tree, he also missed his wombat and his mouse.

Night came softly to the bush. Day sounds went away and

209

secret night sounds filled the air. Tabby heard leaves dropping, damp and quiet, and frogs saying "quaaaaa, quaaaaa"
and insects rubbing their horny knees and elbows together.

The mopoke hoo-hooed from the shadows. Tabby's whiskers bristled.

"Just suppose if that fish were a real fish! That mopoke
might eat it. *My* fish!"

Tabby streaked down the trunk of the tree. Two round
orange lamps were glowing at him. The mopoke was already
perched on the fish.

Tabby made a noise like a boiling kettle.

"That's my fish! My friend Wombat caught it just for me.
You leave it alone, you old owl!"

The mopoke liked the fish and wanted it for himself. He
plunged at Tabby and beat him around the ears with his soft
furry wings. Tabby made a furious sound and darted behind
the mopoke.

During this time Wombat was sitting up in bed with his
hat on, gloomily eating some beetles. He wasn't happy because
he no longer had a Tabby Cat for a friend. All at once he
heard angry noises from the garden. Tabby was shrieking and
wailing, and a mopoke was hooting and screeching. Wombat
didn't wait to awaken Mouse. He trundled out to the pine
tree. There was Tabby dancing up and down in a terrible
rage.

"That bird is eating my fish!"

He flickered up the tree so that he could have a better
view. The mopoke made an angry sound.

"Don't you squawk to me like that, you old owl," growled
Wombat. "And that's my Tabby's fish. Don't you touch a
beakful of it!"

The mopoke didn't like wombats, either. He flapped away
from the fish and settled on Wombat's hat. He held on with
his claws and whacked with his beak and his wings. Luckily
the hat was large, and Wombat had a hard head. He wasn't

hurt. But he was annoyed. He thought it must surely be bad manners for a bird to sit on his head without being asked. Wombat had been taught about bad manners by Mouse, who was particular.

"It's very uncomfortabubble, you know," he complained.

Tabby dived from the tree. There were cat squeals and bird squawks. There was a great scurry of flapping wings. Then the mopoke untangled himself and flew off in a flurry.

"Tabby, you brave cat, you chased him away!"

"Eating my fish, pecking my wombat—some mopokes are just so hard to put up with!" gasped Tabby. He thought he might faint, but he didn't have time.

Wombat beamed. He hugged Tabby and almost flattened him.

"Hero cat! Wait till Mouse hears!"

"Just wait!" gasped Tabby.

"You're the bestest cat in the whole of Big Bush!" said Wombat excitedly, squeezing harder.

"Air, air!" panted Tabby.

Wombat let him go. "Aw, you're all squozen, poor Tab," said Wombat, trying to push his friend back into shape. "And Mouse and I are so sorry we bothered you about the treehouse, Tab! It was very bad of us to pester such a wonderful cat."

"Handsome, too," added Tabby, who was getting his breath back.

"And we're never, never going to bother you again because you're a hero cat and fight mopokes."

Tabby was so thrilled that he was not going to be bothered any more that at once he invited Mouse and Wombat to tea on the following day.

"The treehouse will be finished, and the door will be painted, and perhaps I shall cook some cakes in my dolls' stove. *Do* come, Wombat," said Tabby, overcome with gladness because they were all friends again. He added: "You *will* have clean paws, Wombat?"

Wombat said he would.

"And wear your new cardigan, and comb your whiskers, and be sure you have a clean hanky."

"No, can't have a clean hanky," explained Wombat, "because it got lost. But I have a terribubbly nice rag."

"I will not have visitors with rag hankies, I will not!" screamed Tabby. "You come with a proper hanky or you're not coming at all. And be sure to make a fuss about how beautiful the treehouse is, or I'll send you right home again."

Mouse was happy when it heard that they were all friends

again. It made sure that Wombat washed his muddy paws, and it made him take his Christmas hanky, the one with a koala in the corner.

"We must be very polite, Wombat dear, and squeak only when we're squoken to. And oh, Wombat, please be careful when you're climbing the ladder!"

Wombat said he would. He knew more about ladders now. Still, he thought it was very silly to have so many holes between the rungs. Anyone could fall through them, he said. So, though Mouse was riding in Wombat's hat, it was very jumpy until it reached the treehouse.

The treehouse! Oh, how little and secret it was! There it stood amongst the leaves, firm and square on its little platform. Its door was as new and glossy as a boiled lolly. A tiny brass knocker in the shape of a fish hung by its tail on the door. A large letterbox was fixed to a nearby branch. There was a notice on it. The notice said: MAIL. T. CAT ESQ.

Mouse was longing to knock with the fish knocker, but it knew that Wombat was longing too.

"A quiet, well-bred tap, please Wombat dear."

Wombat took the little fish in his paddy paw. He banged both paw and knocker against the door. There was a thunderous sound, and the door fell down. Tabby, who had been wait-

ing impatiently to let in his guests, was wearing a smart, bright ski cap and a shocked look.

Mouse didn't know what to say. It was very sorry for Tabby, but it felt it had to stand by its wombat.

"Oh, Tabby, what a shame! Wombat didn't mean to do it, really he didn't."

"Everything happens to me," wailed Tabby brokenly.

"Wombat will fix it for you, won't you, Wombat dear?" asked Mouse, giving Wombat a sharp nip on the ear, which was handy.

Wombat nodded. A tear rolled down his flat, black leather nose. To think he had done such a terrible thing! When Tabby saw the tear he forgave Wombat at once.

"Well, come in, you animals. Don't let the cakes go to waste."

Wombat and Mouse stepped in very carefully. Full of admiration, they stared about the treehouse. They saw the window, and the blue curtains. They saw the polished floor and the warm rug with a design of cats and kittens. Mouse saw the dolls' stove with the fire sparkling like red stars through the grate. Mouse saw the rack with pretty plates and cups and bowls, and another little shelf which bore Tabby's beauty aids, paw lotion and things like that.

Wombat saw the cakes arranged on a dish. Some had delicious squiggles of chocolate. Some had cherries. Some had nuts.

"Oh, Tabby," said Mouse and Wombat together. "You *are* smart!"

Tabby felt a little better.

"Just the same, don't think you're going to live here," he said. "You're just visiting. Have a cake, Wombat!"

Wombat made a glad noise and forgot all his manners. He rushed at the cake dish. There was a great sound of breaking wood, and he fell through the floor. With his elbows propped at the sides of the hole he looked shyly at Tabby.

"Aw, look what I've done. I don't suppose you've noticed, Tab, but I've gone through the floor. I'm stuck."

Tabby pulled the ski cap over his eyes and face. Mouse bounced up and down trying to comfort him.

"Oh, Tabby, don't cry. Oh, Tabby, we're so sorry. Please, dear Tabby, say you don't mind?"

Tabby began to mutter in a low, fast, nervous voice: "Only this morning I was a carefree cat with a treehouse. Now I'm a broken-down cat with a wombat stuck in the middle of the

floor for ever. For how does a person get a wombat out of the floor? Push him down? Pull him up? He's too fat for that. He hasn't enough corners to hold on to. Oh, I'm a poor unlucky pussy, and I might as well go and jump in the creek and get wet paws."

"May I have a cake, please?" asked Wombat. "One with a cherry."

"You don't seem at all worried, Wombat," scolded Mouse. "Don't you understand? You might be stuck there for ever."

"Treely ruly?" Wombat thought for a while. "Then I'd better have two cakes."

Tabby went outside to see how much damage had been caused. He saw Wombat's short fat legs dangling down through the leaves. At first he thought that he might bite them, then he remembered that he was a well brought-up cat. Sadly he climbed back. Wombat was beaming sunnily around and eating his fourth cake.

"I like it here, it's cosy," he announced.

"Mouse, make him climb out; go on, Mouse," pleaded Tabby.

Mouse shook its head gloomily.

"I've tried already, poor dear Tabby. He says he doesn't mind being stuck in the floor."

"It's comfortabubble, you know," said Wombat.

"Very well," said Mouse grimly. "I hope you like it when you're here all by yourself tonight. That mopoke will have a wonderful time pecking your toes."

"And it will likely snap off your tail," added Tabby helpfully. "If you call that silly little tuft of nothing a tail."

"Poor Wombat," sighed Mouse. "What a sight he'll look in the morning."

"This time I'd like a cake with a squiggle, please," said Wombat. He thought while he ate it, and then he said: "All right. I'll try to get out. But you'll have to help, you know."

Mouse took charge at once. It gave the orders and Tabby

did the work. Tabby pulled at Wombat's paws until his grey nose turned quite purple, and his tongue stuck out.

"Why can't I play, too?" complained Wombat. Tabby stopped pulling and wailed with rage.

"He isn't heaving, he isn't trying a bit, Mouse. He's just sitting there like a great fat lump while I do all the work. Now, Wombat, when I say one, two, three, you *heave*."

Tabby said one, two, three, and began to pull again.

"I like you with your tongue out, Tab," said Wombat admiringly. "It's such a pretty little tongue, like a rose petal."

Tabby was charmed. He left off pulling and looked at his tongue in a looking-glass.

"You know, it *is* like a rose petal. You're not such a muddle-head after all."

Mouse said a few stern words about Tabby's tongue. Then it pointed downwards.

"You get down on the ladder, Tabby, and push. And I'll pull."

Tabby went. He leaned from the ladder and pushed hard at Wombat's brown back. His nose turned purple again. Even his rose-petal tongue turned purple. Wombat did not move an inch. Instead, the rest of the floor gave way and he fell to the ground.

"Oh, Wombat, are you hurt?" squeaked Mouse, popping out the treehouse door.

"No," said Wombat, "it's very comfortabubble because I fell on a useful cushion, Mouse."

Mouse noticed at once that one end of the useful cushion had a tail. It scampered down to help. Tabby wasn't *quite* flat, but he was not looking himself. He said he wasn't strong enough for wombats, and could well do without mice, and all he wanted to do was to go to bed in his dear little treehouse.

Wombat wanted very much to be kind to his friend. Besides, he thought happily, if Tabby had broken something, such as a neck, he and Mouse could have a delightful time playing doctors. He draped Tabby around his neck like a fur, grabbed Mouse, and lumbered up the ladder into the treehouse. He dropped Tabby on his bed. At once the middle of

the bed collapsed, the two ends closed up, and all that could be seen of Tabby Cat was one paw and the end of his tail.

"My!" marvelled Mouse. "What a strange bed. Tabby must have invented it himself. He *does* sound angry, doesn't he, Wombat?"

Wombat untangled the bed. Tabby was so bad tempered that he couldn't get a word out. That suited Wombat and Mouse very well. Mouse fetched him a hot water bottle and

made him some lemonade while Wombat mended the broken
door and the hole in the floor. Mouse stroked Tabby's head
and brushed his whiskers and soon he was able to sit up and
feebly eat a sardine.

"I'll be cross with you both later," he promised.

"Yes, you do that, Tabby," said kind little Mouse.

It was delightful in the treehouse, with the wind blowing
gently through the window and good smells of leaves and bark
all around. The whole house rocked gently like a rocking
chair. Tabby felt quite pleased that he had been fallen on.

"Besides, Wombat said my tongue is like a pink rose petal,
and it is, too," he said to himself. "Lucky me!"

CHAPTER III

Cats Need Friends

At first everyone enjoyed Tabby's stay in bed. Tabby liked being looked after and Wombat liked playing doctors, and Mouse liked trotting around the treehouse deciding what changes should be made.

"Pink curtains instead of blue, I think, Tabby dear," said Mouse. "And wouldn't you like my photograph on the wall instead of that horrid picture of a wet sock?"

"That wet sock is my rich Uncle Tom Cat," replied Tabby in a dignified way.

At once Mouse said it was sorry, and Tabby forgave it.

But he turned on one side and pretended to be asleep.

"Now I know what has happened," he whispered. "My dear friends have come to live with me, that's what. I built a treehouse to get away from them, but here they are, as large as life and twice as muddle-headed. Oh everything happens to me!"

Tabby realised he must be cunning. That was the only way to get Wombat and Mouse to go away to their own home and leave him in peace.

"After all," he brooded, "it shouldn't be so hard for a brilliant cat like me. I have more brains than a wombat and Mouse is so small it doesn't matter."

Although Tabby didn't know it, Mouse was standing on his pillow. It was carrying an eggcup of hot cocoa as a little treat for Tabby. When it heard Tabby muttering these mysterious things, Mouse thought for a moment that it might pour the cocoa into Tabby's ear, which was sticking out from under the blanket. But Mouse knew that would be unkind.

Besides, it wanted to creep quietly away so that Tabby wouldn't know it had heard.

Mouse's feelings were hurt. It blotted up a tear with the end of its tail.

"Just imagine," it thought. "Tabby doesn't want us to live with him. Oh, how ungrateful! But he's only a cat; he doesn't know any better. I mustn't let him do anything he'd be sorry for, poor Tabby. I'm his friend, after all."

All day Tabby didn't say anything about his plans. Then he saw his chance for getting Wombat and Mouse out of the treehouse. Mouse had noticed that the treehouse hadn't a bath.

"Well, you see, Mouse, cats don't need one. As long as a cat has his paws and his rose petal tongue, he's a clean cat."

"All very well," replied Mouse briskly, "but mice like proper baths with soap and a face washer, and a small brush for toenails. Let me see, what can I use for a bath?"

"I know," said Tabby. "There's a very good old pie dish in our house on the ground, Mouse. You could bring it to the treehouse."

"But I couldn't carry a pie dish, Tabby dear," cried Mouse.

"Of course not, pretty little Mouse," beamed Tabby, "so you must take big, strong Wombat to help you."

Wombat was very pleased. Though he loved the treehouse, he also loved to trundle around in the sunshine and roll in the mud and rub wet leaves on his face.

"We'll hurry back, so that you won't be lonely, dear old Tab," he promised.

"Yes, *do*, Wombat," said Tabby. Mouse shook its head sadly at Tabby's cunning, but no one noticed.

"Are you all safe in my pocket, Mouse?" asked Wombat as he began to climb down the ladder. But Mouse was not in Wombat's pocket. Mouse had twinkled into Tabby's new ski cap, which was lying on the floor.

Tabby went to the door. He saw Wombat's broad, brown back waggling away through the trees. Tabby did a little dance of joy. He banged the red door and bolted it. He put on his cosy ski cap.

"Hooray, hooray, I've my little house to myself again! Oh, I'm so clever! I deserve a salmon sandwich, I really do."

A sad little voice spoke from somewhere up in the air.

"Tabby, Tabby," it sighed. "I'm ashamed of you!"

Tabby dropped the tin opener. He stood like a frozen cat. "Who . . . who was that?" he quavered.

"I am a goblin Mouse," said the voice. "Oh, Tabby, you

turned your best friends out into the snow. How could you do such a wicked thing, Tabby?"

"Is it really snowing out there?" whimpered Tabby. "I thought it was sunny."

"It doesn't matter a bit. Don't be stupid!" snapped the voice. "You don't want your best friends to live with you. You're a catty old cat, and I'm going to pull your eyebrows."

Mouse was sitting on top of Tabby's head, rather squashed because the ski cap was full of ears. It reached forward and gave one of Tabby's eyebrows a smart tug. Tabby leaped like a frog. He had no sooner come back to earth before the other eyebrow was tweaked. He put up a shaking paw. Nothing and nobody! No one was touching his eyebrows.

"Oh, it is, it is, it *is* a goblin!" whimpered Tabby.

"A mischievous goblin, too," corrected the voice. "I'm going to pull your whiskers now and don't you deserve it?"

Tabby shrieked and clapped both paws over his much-loved whiskers. Mouse, who was dangling down from the edge of the ski cap, scuttled back just in time. But first it managed to give one whisker a good tweak.

"Go away, go away, goblin Mouse!" begged poor Tabby. "I'm a nervous little pussy and my fur will turn white if you don't."

"Oh, good," replied Mouse heartlessly. "I do like white cats. I think I'll stay in the treehouse and haunt you for ever."

Just then there was a great commotion outside. It was Wombat beating the pie dish on the treehouse door.

"Tabby, Tabby, open the door, I've brought you a surprise!"

"There," said the goblin Mouse. "That's the kindhearted animal you've shut outside in the cold. Open the door, you mean old Tab, you."

This time Tabby was rat-tatted on the head by four goblin paws. With a squeak of terror he opened the door. Wombat, who had been leaning against it, toppled in with the pie dish.

There was so much commotion that Mouse had plenty of time to creep down Tabby's back and into Wombat's pocket. As soon as the noise had stopped, it sauntered out, looking bright and cheerful.

"Why, Tabby dear, what are you doing on the floor? You should be in bed, you poor, pale pussy."

"Of course he should," said Wombat, seizing Tabby by the tail and bearing him tenderly towards the bed. He flung

Tabby into bed and dragged up the blankets. Tabby's feet were left sticking out at the bottom.

"I've a headache," whispered Tabby pitifully.

"Would you like a nice, cold sardine on your hot old head, because the surprise I brought is a tin of sardines?"

Tabby said no, not really.

"I know, I'll sing you a bubbalye and you can go to sleep!" said Wombat eagerly.

"I'd rather have a bedtime story, thank you, Wombat," said Tabby. Wombat was pleased. He loved telling stories.

"Do you want little Red Riding Wolf, or Cindergorilla?"

"No, no, Wombat dear," said Mouse. "Tell Tabby a sooth-ing little story about a kitten. One that is suitable for a sick cat. And *I* shall go and have my bath."

Tabby felt a little more cheerful. He could, after all, try some other time to get Wombat and Mouse to leave the tree-house. And perhaps, if he was good for a little while, the gob-lin Mouse might drift off and bother the mopoke instead.

He sat up in bed waiting for his bedtime story.

"Once upon a time," began Wombat, "there was a nice little kitten and he was walking down a long, dark street."

"Yes, and then what?" asked Tabby timidly.

"Something jumped out at him from behind the garbage tin!"

"Good gracious!" said Tabby faintly.

"And something grabbed him, something with claws!" said Wombat. Tabby fell back on his pillow.

"Mouse, Mouse!" he moaned.

Mouse scampered to his side. It was wearing a very small pink dressing gown.

"Oh, that poor kitten," wailed Tabby. "I shall never forget those claws, never!"

"It was only his old mother cat," said Wombat crossly, "come to fetch him home, and they were going to have pancakes for tea and everything. You've spoiled my story, silly ole Tabby."

"Imagine frightening Tabby like that!" said Mouse sternly. "I expect he'll lie awake all night. You ought to be ashamed of yourself, Wombat!"

However, in spite of his fright, Tabby fell asleep before Mouse had finished scolding Wombat. Mouse tucked the blankets around him and tiptoed away. It had thought of some new stern things to say to Wombat, but he was already asleep. He had curled up in the corner like a hairy, brown rug. Mouse had its bath. It was sitting in its pyjamas rubbing cold cream on its nose, when suddenly Tabby rose from his bed.

Mouse couldn't believe its eyes, so it put on its spectacles. Tabby walked stiffly, like a wound-up cat. He stalked past Mouse and opened the door.

"Oh, Tabby, don't look like that. You make me feel so creepy," gasped Mouse.

Tabby's eyes were wide open and his rose-petal tongue was sticking out. Mouse realised he was walking in his sleep.

"Oh, it must have been that frightening bedtime story Wombat told him," said Mouse. "Tabby, don't go out there. You might fall!"

There was a bad-tempered hoot, and Tabby flew back

inside with something feathery and yellow-eyed after him. By now Tabby was wide-awake, and that was lucky, for he shut the door just in time.

"Oh, Tabby," cried Mouse, hugging its friend's knee. "That owl was outside waiting for you. What a narrow escape!"

"But how did I get there?" wondered Tabby. "I thought I was in bed! Oh, Mouse, whatever has happened to your dear pussy?"

Mouse explained. Tabby was thrilled to think he had been walking in his sleep. He thought it was unusual and rather exciting. Still, he saw how it could be dangerous.

"Just suppose, I might wander off and bite a dog, or anything!" he said proudly. "We must take great care that I don't do it again."

Wombat was still snoring, so Tabby awakened him and told him what had happened. Wombat was furious that he had missed the sight of the mopoke chasing Tabby. Still, he agreed that he and Mouse should take turns watching Tabby so that he didn't walk in his sleep again.

"Who will be first?" asked Tabby.

"Wombat, because he's the fattest," said Mouse smartly. "Well, good night, Tabby dear."

Off it went. Tabby was left with Wombat, who sat on the floor and held his back paws with his front ones and rocked to and fro.

"I know I'll never be able to go to sleep," complained Tabby.

"You could count wombats jumping over a fence," suggested Wombat.

Tabby said that would more likely give him a nightmare.

"Then I'll sit on you," said Wombat.

This alarmed Tabby so much that he closed his eyes at once.

Wombat tiptoed to the bed. He pulled up Tabby's eyelid and looked in.

"Are you asleep, Tab, eh? Eh, Tab?"

Tabby opened his eyes. He seized his eggcup of cocoa, which Mouse had left beside his bed, and which was now cold and curdled and horrid, and poured it all over Wombat.

"What a horribubble thing to do," said Wombat, very upset. "It may be all right for cats to have cold cocoa poured all over their cardigans, but wombats are fussy."

"How do you know I'm not still asleep?" asked Tabby, very crossly. Wombat gave a snort of sorrow. Of course that was why Tabby had done it!

"What a mean Wombat I am. I treely ruly almost got cross

with you, Tabby. And you were asleep all the time and didn't know what you were doing."

Tabby felt very ashamed.

"I'm a wicked cat, that's what. I'm not asleep at all, Wombat."

"Of course you are," said Wombat. "You don't know whether you're asleep or awake. How could you, when you're asleep?"

Tabby didn't know what to think. Perhaps he was asleep after all.

"I'll tell you what, Tabby," said helpful Wombat. "I'll put a string around your leg and tie it to the bedpost. Then you won't be able to get away."

Tabby thought that was a good idea.

"Now you go to sleep in your bed, Tabby, and I'll go to sleep too, just to keep you company."

In a moment they were asleep. The mopoke swooped about the treehouse. All was quiet. A long time afterwards, Tabby sat up. His eyes were open, but he was fast asleep. He undid the knot in the string. He slunk silently towards the door and went out.

The mopoke squawked. Tabby woke up and fell off the branch. The string around his leg caught in a twig. He dangled there for a moment before Wombat and Mouse rushed out.

"Save him, Wombat!" cried Mouse, nipping into the letter-box in case the mopoke saw it.

Wombat hauled Tabby up like a fish on the end of the string. Tabby was not choked, but he had not enjoyed it.

"Goodness, Tabby dear," said Mouse, when they were all safe inside the treehouse. "You *do* need us to look after you, don't you?"

The mopoke fluttered silently against the window. Tabby trembled.

"Oh, yes, Mouse, I do need you."

He meant it, too.

CHAPTER IV

The Very Big Storm

THE next morning Wombat rolled out of bed and across the floor. Then he rolled back again. On the way back he met Mouse, also rolling.

"My," remarked Mouse, as they passed, "what a big wind! The treehouse is shaking like anything."

Wombat *was* excited. He looked out the window. He saw the branches swaying and the leaves fluttering. He saw the tops of the trees shivering in the wind.

"I think there's going to be a storm!" he beamed. It seemed to Wombat very good fun to be in a little treehouse while a storm shook the tree like a feather duster.

Mouse wasn't quite so sure. It said it would hurry up and prepare breakfast before things became too rough. It scurried about and clinked its tiny, bright saucepans, and before very long it was serving breakfast.

"Pancakes for you, Tabby dear. And snails for you, Wombat. Ugh!"

It sat down, dabbed some honey on its pancake and looked brightly at Tabby. Tabby was gloomy. He was a worried cat. Mouse smiled.

"Don't worry, Tabby dear. I've thought of a way to cure you of sleepwalking!"

Tabby was grateful.

"Really, Mouse? Because I don't want to sleepwalk any more. I might hurt my wonderful self."

"It's called the Mouse Cure," explained Mouse. "We'll put the pie dish full of water beside your bed, you see. When you step out to go sleepwalking, you'll step in the water and wake up."

"But I'll get my paws wet," complained Tabby. "Just imagine waking up with four wet paws!"

"But you wouldn't like to go sleepwalking in a storm, Tab," pointed out Wombat. "You'll get all your other paws wet, then. How uncomfortabubble!"

He took another snail and put honey on it, just to try. Tabby sighed. He didn't bother to explain that he had no other paws to get wet. After all, Wombat couldn't count past four, so it didn't matter. Tabby saw that Mouse was right. His sleepwalking would have to be cured.

The more he thought about the Mouse Cure, the more he longed for evening to come so that he could try it.

All day long the tree moved uneasily in the little winds that scampered before the big one. Leaves swirled around the treehouse like smoke. Little birds danced past. They were looking for safe shelter before the storm came. A possum

scratched over the treehouse roof and squeezed into a crack in the tree.

At teatime the wind dropped for a while. The moon shone. The shadow of the mopoke flapped across the window and was gone.

"I'll take care he doesn't get a peck at me again," said Tabby. He sighed. "I wonder why he doesn't like me? Everyone else loves me. Well, I do, anyway."

He bustled around and made things ready for the night.

"I've filled the pie dish with water, and there it is beside my bed. Mind you don't fall in it, Mouse! Good night all!"

Mouse and Tabby had forgotten that where there's a wombat there's often a muddle. And there was. Wombat awoke in the night and felt thirsty.

The moonlight showed a big dish full of fresh clean water beside Tabby's bed.

"That Tabby is the bestest cat a wombat ever had," said

Wombat. He had forgotten about the Mouse Cure. All he thought was that his kind friend Tabby had known he would feel thirsty in the night. Wombat trundled over and drank all the water. He carefully licked around the dish so that not a drop remained. Mouse had trained him to be a tidy wombat. Then he went back to bed.

In the middle of the night Tabby grew restless. He kicked and tossed and jumped. The mopoke hooted beyond the window, and every time he hooted, Tabby jumped again. In his dreams he felt that he must get out of bed and run away.

Suddenly Mouse and Wombat were awakened by the crash of a cat falling into an empty pie dish.

"Oh, Tabby dear!" squeaked Mouse. "Are you hurt?"

"Not at all," replied Tabby bitterly. "Just dented all over, that's all."

"He's still asleep, Tabby is," said Wombat.

"No, I'm not," screamed Tabby. "I'm wide-awake. I'm a

wide-awake, battered cat, and my tail is ruined for ever."

Wombat looked at the tail. It seemed more knotty than usual. Wombat longed to help.

"I'm sure I can bend it straight again, treely ruly!"

Tabby tried to get under the bed, but Wombat hauled him out and straightened his tail. After Tabby had finished screaming he looked at his tail. There was only a small kink in the end which Tabby thought rather saucy. He decided to forgive Wombat.

Meanwhile Mouse had been staring at Tabby.

"It's a very strange thing, Tabby dear. You fell in a dish of water and you're not a bit wet. H'm. Now, where could that water have gone?"

It trotted over to Wombat, who was bashfully pulling his hat over his eyes.

"Bend over, Wombat," ordered Mouse. "H'm," it said. "Just as I thought. Wet whiskers!"

Still, falling into the pie dish had been such a shock for

Tabby that he was cured of sleepwalking. This was just as well, because the treehouse was beginning to rock and sway once more. Outside, the air was full of creaks and squeaks and roarings as the wind swooped down upon Big Bush.

Mouse and Tabby clung to Wombat and looked at each other wide-eyed. (They could cling to Wombat because he was so short and stumpy, rather like a piece of very solid furniture.) Wombat *was* enjoying the storm.

"I'm pretending the treehouse is a ship. It's called Noah's Bark. Why did Noah bark?"

"Well, never mind," said Mouse hurriedly. It joined in the game quickly. "Let's sail off to some wonderful country full of adventures."

"And fish?" asked Tabby anxiously.

"Lots of fish, I'm sure," said Mouse.

"Well, I don't want any," announced Tabby. "I'm treesick."

He staggered off. When he was getting into bed he fell in

the pie dish once again, but he took no notice at all.

"My," said Mouse, "he really must feel queer. Well, you and I will have fun, won't we, Wombat? I'll be the ship's cook and you can be the captain."

But Wombat didn't want to be the captain. He said the cook had more fun. The captain never had a chance to put his paw into saucepans and have a little lick, Wombat said.

Mouse said he could be the ship's cook's helper.

Daylight was coming. It was not bright daylight. The clouds had sailed down over the bush, and the trees had bent down over the treehouse and shut all the light out. The treehouse bumped up and down. It dipped this way and that, and the branches banged on its roof. Tabby lay still and whimpered, but the ship's cook and the ship's cook's helper were feeling very healthy.

By now all the cakes that Tabby had prepared when he invited them to visit him had gone. Mouse said it would cook some more that evening. Wombat found some peanuts in a tin. He rocked across the floor and looked at suffering Tabby. Tabby made a long, pitiful caterwaul.

"I know. Tabby wants a peanut," said Wombat.

Tabby opened his mouth to say he didn't want anything

but peace and quiet, and Wombat promptly posted the peanut.

All day long the storm blew. Suddenly there was a great bang. Mouse thought the roof had blown off. Wombat thought the tree was falling down. Treesick Tabby dashed out of bed, leaped to the top of Wombat's head, which was near the window just then, and looked out.

"The ladder has blown down! We're marooned!"

"Just like shipwrecked sailors," said Mouse, not knowing whether to be thrilled or frightened.

"I know, I know, like Robinson Crucat!" roared Wombat, and he lay down on the floor and kicked with excitement. But Mouse took a sterner view.

"Tabby, you go right down there and put that ladder up again," it commanded.

"Me?" quavered Tabby. "Out in that storm? A frail little thing like me?"

"But you're the only climbing animal," said Mouse.

"Perhaps I am, but I'm a delicate climbing animal as well," objected Tabby. "I might get pneumonia. A branch might fall on me. The mopoke might catch me. My paws might get soaked. Anything might happen."

He looked defiantly at Mouse.

"Don't you bully me, Mouse. I'll go when the storm dies down and not a moment before."

"Of all the selfish cats!" boiled Mouse.

But it was no use. Tabby staggered back to bed (for the floor was tilting this way and that, just like a ship's deck, and not even a person with four feet could walk easily). Wombat was delighted.

"Don't be cross, Mouse. Let's be three Robinson Crucats and have a lovely time. Please, Mouse?"

Mouse giggled. "All right. We shall make the best of it. I shall cook a delicious tea. What shall we have?"

"Snails," said Wombat.

"I know," said Mouse. "I'll bake a pie."

It climbed up on Wombat's head, which this time was near the cupboard, and opened the door. It squeaked with dismay.

"There's nothing in here. The cupboard is bare!"

"Treely ruly? Just like Old Mother Cupboard?"

Wombat thought that all his favourite stories were coming

true. He waggled his paws up and down, for that helped him
to remember, and sang:

"Old Mother Cupboard went to the hubbard

To get her poor frog a bone."

"Oh, do be quiet, like a good animal," said Mouse. "I'm
very worried. Tabby dear, where is all the food?"

"There isn't any," said Tabby. "Just a few tins of sardines
for me."

Mouse made a speech about sardines being all right for
thoughtless cats who never considered their dear friends, but
what were the dear friends going to eat?

"I had some flour and honey and milk and sugar and you
made pancakes with them," explained Tabby. "Besides, I
didn't expect my dear friends to come and live with me, or
the ladder to be blown down, or anything. Oh, everything
happens to me, it isn't fair!"

Mouse knew that what Tabby said was true.

"Well, never mind," it said. "We're not very hungry yet.

Tomorrow the storm may have blown away, and Tabby can climb down and put up the ladder and we'll be able to go out and get some food."

"I'm hungry right now," grumbled Wombat.

He began to hunt around the treehouse. He found one cold pancake which Mouse said it would die rather than eat. He found two snails that had come in out of the storm. He found three peanuts and an old second-hand sweet. It had once been striped red and white but now it was grey all over. Mouse said it would die rather than eat that, too.

"I'm going to put it away safely, just the same," said Wombat.

"It looks as though I'm going to be the only shipwrecked sailor," said Mouse rather dismally.

It put on a very noble expression as it set the table with two places. Tabby had sardines and Wombat had the snails. Mouse ate a cake crumb and half a peanut. It was hungry, but it was a brave Mouse and didn't complain.

"Of course, the storm will be over soon," it promised itself. "And then what a dinner I shall have. Three mosquitoes, I wouldn't be surprised."

"*Do* have a snail," Wombat pleaded. "You've no idea how terribubbly tasty they are."

Mouse said it didn't want to find out.

"Anyway," it said, "it's much worse for that poor mopoke. He's outside in the rain and the cold. At least we're cosy."

They told each other stories until it was time to go to bed.

In the morning the tree was still tossing. Lakes of water lay all around. The possum scurried away down a branch, its fur sodden and its tail like a wet duster. Tabby had sardines for breakfast and Wombat had the other two peanuts. Mouse had another cake crumb.

"We must play a game so that we won't think of food all the time," said Tabby. "I've an idea for an interesting one. Look, Wombat, look, Mouse, what does this remind you of?"

He put his ski cap on at a dashing angle, with the tassel falling over one eye. Wombat and Mouse stared at him thoughtfully.

"I'm sorry, Tabby dear," said Mouse at last. "You just look like a cat who doesn't know where his eyes are."

Tabby miaowed with rage. "I'm a pirate, I'm a pirate!"

"No, Tabby," explained Wombat kindly. "You can't be because pirates wear blue caps and drive planes."

"That's a pilot, Wombat," said Mouse. "Yes, I see what you mean, Tabby dear. Well, perhaps we could play pirates. Pirates," it added helpfully to Wombat, "are bad sea robbers with wooden legs."

Wombat stuck out his lip. "Then I can't be a pirate. My legs are all made of wombat."

"Only some pirates have wooden legs, muddle-head," said Tabby.

"Of course, we won't be bad pirates," said Mouse, "we'll be *good* pirates. You be Captain Blackbeard, Tabby, and I'll be . . . let me see . . ."

"You can be Horribubble," suggested Wombat.

Mouse said it certainly wouldn't. It would be plain Mouse first.

"All right, Plain Mouse," said Wombat. "Then I'll be Horribubble. What shall we do first?"

"Something bold and daring," said Plain Mouse. Then it sighed. "Of course, Horribubble dear, you and I can't be the *most* brave and daring. Captain Blackbeard is the boldest and bravest with his handsome red cap and everything."

"*Why* should old Blackfeet be the bravest?" growled Wombat jealously. "He isn't the bravest. He's only the skinniest."

Tabby flew into a rage. He strutted around looking fierce and twirling his whiskers.

"Of course I'm the bravest as well as the handsomest. Now, let me see, what can I do to prove to this muddle-head that I deserve to be captain of this pirate ship?"

"Jump off?" suggested Wombat. Tabby gave him a proud sneer.

"After all, I'm the boldest pirate on the seven seas. It will have to be something good."

"You could go out into the storm and put the ladder up," suggested Mouse. "Oh, Captain Blackbeard, will you? You're so strong and fearless. What would we do without you?"

CHAPTER V

Do Wombats Ever Fly?

O F course Mouse was having fun with Tabby. It really
didn't mean to tease him into going outside. When
Tabby gave it a wonderful look of sorrow and terror,
Mouse scampered over and playfully bit him on the toe.

"Oh, Captain Blackbeard, I was only joking!"

"We wouldn't want you to go out into the storm, treely
ruly, dear old Captain Blackfoot," said Horribubble the
pirate, "even though we are starving hungry and I'll sit on
you if you don't."

"You stop talking that way, Horribubble!" Plain Mouse
frowned. It believed in kindness to cats. But, to its surprise,
Captain Blackbeard drew himself up proudly and said in a

246

hero's voice: "You all think I'm a coward. Even if I am, you shouldn't tell me so. I *will* go out and put the ladder up. So there!"

"But Captain, it's still raining."

Plain Mouse was upset that its joke had been taken seriously.

"Don't go, Tab," begged Wombat. "Stay here and we'll play cannibubbles instead. Do cannibubbles eat cats? Eh?"

Horribubble looked so very hungry that Captain Blackbeard felt nervous. It seemed to him that it was as dangerous to stay in the treehouse as to go out. He marched towards the door. His paws trembled a little, but he managed to say in a grand, solemn way: "If I don't come back I leave all my belongings to my best friends, Mouse and Wombat."

At once Plain Mouse and Horribubble turned back into their usual selves. Mouse burst into tears. Wombat plumped down on the floor and pulled his hat over his eyes.

"Don't go, Tabby dear!" they cried.

Tabby flung open the door. It shut behind him. Wombat and Mouse rushed to the window. Mouse scurried up to the top of Wombat's head.

"I can't see him *anywhere*! Oh, brave Tabby, where are you?"

"Heeeeeelp, heeeeeelp! Someone save a poor cat!"

Someone scratched at the door. There was a feathery thump.

"The mopoke!" growled Wombat.

"He's chasing Tabby!" cried Mouse. "Open the door, Wombat!"

Wombat was so anxious to help poor Tabby that he gave the door a great tug. It flew open and Tabby, who had been flattened up against it like a bookmark, fell in. Wombat looked around. He could not see the mopoke. He shut the door.

"He's gone back into the letterbox!" panted Tabby. "My letterbox! Oh, Mouse, what a fright your handsome pussy

had when he flapped out after me. Just imagine, I expected lovely airletters and little presents in my letterbox, and instead I have an owl. It's not a bit fair!"

"You're just a poor old pirate," soothed Mouse.

"No, I'm not, Mouse. I'm just Tabby, and I *am* a coward, Mouse. Oh, why am I me? Nobody loves me!"

"We love you terribubbly, don't we, Mouse?" said Wombat.

"But whatever shall we do without the ladder?" hiccuped Tabby. "We mightn't get out of the treehouse for days."

Mouse polished its glasses and laughed in an adventurous way.

"Well, we won't worry. There are lots of things to eat yet. There's half a sardine, and Wombat's horrid grey sweet, and goodness knows what else! Let's see what we can find."

So they turned out all their pockets. Tabby had some dust in the corners of his, and Mouse, as it was so tidy, did not even have dust. Wombat had some little knobbles of wool that no one could eat except a moth, and a queer brown woody thing that turned out to be a corner of ginger biscuit.

They had a jolly meal. Mouse was so gay that Tabby cheered up, and Wombat was always cheerful anyway. Tabby had the sardine, and Wombat had the wooden biscuit, and Mouse had the cold pancake, which was very dreadful and tasted like buttered balloon.

All night the storm raged about the treehouse. The next

morning there was still a sad, grey sky and a cold wind. They drew straws for the horrid grey lolly and Tabby won. He said everything happened to him, and it had. The sweet was too hard for his teeth and he had to throw it out the window.

By the time evening came they were all very grumpy. Mouse kept thinking of delicious dinners of mosquitoes and grass seeds, and Tabby wept a tear or two as he dreamed of fish pie and a cod liver oil milk-shake to follow. Wombat just grumbled to himself. He looked about the treehouse. An animal couldn't eat saucepans or blankets or curtains. But there must be something to eat, something that no wombat had ever thought of eating before.

Wombat noticed the little shelf beside the looking glass. There was Tabby's paw lotion, and one or two other bottles.

"What's that?" asked Wombat, giving one of the bottles a poke.

"Oh, that's my Furgro," explained Tabby. "It's a hair tonic."

"May I rub some on top of my head where it's moulted be-

cause Mouse stamps around when it's riding in my hat?" asked Wombat.

"Of course you can't!" said Tabby crossly.

"Why can't I have just a little spread on a gumleaf?" asked Wombat sadly. "I'm just so hungry I can't bear it any more, treely ruly." He picked up a little green bottle. "But perhaps this tastes better. Does it, Mouse?"

Mouse read the label. "It's Miaow, the Perfume for Particular Pussies."

"Then I'll have a spoonful of that," said Wombat.

Tabby grabbed the bottle and held it to his chest. "Oh, please don't eat my Miaow!"

Mouse ran up Wombat's chest and tapped him on his black leather nose.

"You will not eat Tabby's hair tonic and you will not drink his perfume, either. Because those things are not made to eat."

"But I'm starving, Mouse!" said Wombat.

"It doesn't make any difference. You mustn't eat things out of jars or bottles if they aren't food."

"Can boy and girl joeys?" asked Wombat. Mouse gave him another tap on the nose.

"Of course they can't. And they wouldn't, either. They're sensible."

"Then I'll be sensibubble too, because I like boy and girl joeys," said Wombat, and he took the bottle back from the particular pussy (who was very glad) and put it on the shelf.

"And now," announced Mouse, "we shall have a pretend dinner. *That* will be fun."

Tabby didn't think so, and Wombat didn't think so.

"Very well," said Mouse carelessly. "*I* shall have a pretend dinner."

Tabby and Wombat watched with great interest as Mouse set the table, using the prettiest plate, the brightest spoon

and fork. It brushed its ears and whiskers, polished its spectacles, washed its paws and sat down. It began to eat from the empty plate.

"Silly," said Tabby scornfully.

"What are you eating, Mouse?" asked Wombat.

"Jelly and ice cream," replied Mouse.

"Red jelly?" asked Wombat.

"Strawberry," said Mouse. It went on eating. Tabby snorted.

"You've dropped some on your front," pointed out Wombat.

"So I have. Thank you, Wombat dear," said Mouse. It carefully removed a blob of nothing from its pretty white front. Then it went on eating. Wombat felt hungrier than ever.

"I *would* like some jelly and ice cream, Mouse, treely ruly."

"Certainly," said Mouse. "Run and wash your paws."

251

"I've never heard anything so silly in all my nine lives!" cried Tabby. Wombat bounced with joy.

"He doesn't want any pretend jelly and ice cream! May I have his share, too?"

"Well, you can't, you greedy wombat!" squawked Tabby angrily. "Don't you dare give it to him, Mouse! I'll wash my paws and I'll be straight back to eat my jelly and ice cream. The idea . . . one animal having two dinners!"

All the time he was gobbling his pretend dinner, Tabby was glaring at Wombat. He said that some animals didn't care if their second-best friend starved, even if that second-best friend was a golden-hearted and handsome cat. He said that Wombat had spilled some jelly on the tablecloth, and he had ice cream all over his whiskers and he was a disgrace.

"Stop complaining, Tabby dear," said little Mouse, "and eat your apple."

Tabby said that cats didn't like apple.

"That's good," said Wombat, "because I've eaten it."

Tabby felt around the table. There was no apple. He flew into a rage.

"Mouse, that muddle-head has eaten your little cat's apple. Mouse, he took it! Squeak sternly to him, Mouse!"

"I didn't know it was yours," said Wombat. He beamed. "It was the most terribubbly nice pretend apple I ever had."

Just then there was an enormous puff of wind. Timber creaked, nails squawked, and the treehouse came loose from the platform and was blown out of the tree. Mouse vanished into Wombat's cardigan pocket. Tabby forgot about his lost apple and leaped into Wombat's arms.

"We're flying, we are, treely ruly!" shouted Wombat.

And so they were.

Wombat saw leaves whizzing past the window. He saw grey, gloomy cloud and a wink of lightning. He saw the wet possum's piggy nose sticking out of a wet crack in the wet tree.

"My!" said a little voice from Wombat's pocket.

Wombat took Mouse by the tail and turned it the right way up. It was too scared to scold him.

"Bother, bother, bother!" it said. The treehouse landed. It did not land like a plane or a butterfly or a leaf. It landed kerplump.

Wombat sat down in a hurry. Tabby flew out of Wombat's grasp and landed on the shelf beside the looking glass. He was very upset but he could not help noticing how handsome he looked with his eyes so big and black with fright.

"Where are we, Wombat?" whispered Mouse.

Wombat had a look. "Under the willow tree in our garden," he said.

He lifted Mouse so that it could see, too.

"Oh, Wombat," breathed Mouse, "it's the nicest place, with the willow fronds all around like a dear little green curtain. Our treehouse is just like a cubby! Tabby, do come and see!"

Tabby put on a drop of Miaow, and sprang to the window sill. He, too, was very pleased.

"I like the treehouse down here. It doesn't bounce and

sway. It stays still, and that's what a delicate cat needs . . . a peaceful house."

"And the storm has blown away," said Wombat. He could see some raggy, grey edges of cloud fluttering away over the treetops.

Mouse tugged at Tabby's paw.

"We were naughty to come and live with you when you didn't want us. But we missed you, Tab. That's why we did it '

"Please say we can come and live with you in your cubby, Tabby," pleaded Wombat. "We won't stay longer than weeks and weeks, treely ruly we won't."

Tabby knew that he would have been lonely as well as hungry if he had stayed in the treehouse all by himself. He was glad he had had his friends with him during the storm.

"A frail little pussy needs his friends," he said.

Wombat was wondering about the mopoke. He went outside and looked up into the pine tree. Two round eyes like little suns looked down from the letterbox. They had a comfortable look-out from the slit marked T. CAT ESQ.

"He didn't want to hurt us," said Wombat. "He just wanted to chase us out of his pine tree. And now he has a horribubbly nice cubby of his own."

He waved a paw. The mopoke could not see him in the daylight. Wombat didn't mind. He understood about owls.

Mouse was trotting around the cubby and deciding what things should be changed.

"Let's paint the step, Tabby dear. And we must move in two more beds, and clean the window and wash the curtains and shake out that pretty mat with the design of cats and kittens. And Tabby, let's buy lots of things to fill the cupboard. I *do* like full cupboards, don't you?"

Tabby and Wombat realised they felt very hungry. Mouse said it did, too, though of course the pretend dinner had been delicious.

"We can go back to our *big* house and cook a real dinner!" said Wombat. He took Tabby's paws and they did a little dance of joy on the grass which was already beginning to stand up straight again after the rain. Daisies and dandelions showed everywhere. Birds began to chirrup.

"Dinner!" shouted Tabby and Wombat, and they galloped towards their big house.

But Mouse made a daisy chain and trailed it all the way home.

Snugglepot and Cuddlepie

By May Gibbs

This Australian Children's Classic edition of the best-loved children's book brings the adventures of Snugglepot and Cuddlepie to a new generation of Australians. May Gibbs' enchanting bush world, peopled with gumnut heroes and heroines, solid friends like Mr Lizard and Mrs Bear and, of course, the villainous Banksia men, has played an important part in the imaginative background of Australian children.

Children who have not yet made the acquaintance of the Nuts and their friends will welcome this paperback edition. It includes most of the original illustrations, which contribute as much as the stories to the charm, humour and character of May Gibbs' classic.

ISBN 0 207 16730 3

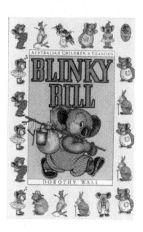

Blinky Bill

By Dorothy Wall

Blinky Bill, the mischievous little Koala, is one of the best-known and best-loved characters in Australian children's fiction. The scrapes and adventures in which naughty Blinky takes such enthusiastic pleasure (to the despair of his mother, Mrs Koala), and the bush creatures he meets along the way, have made these stories firm favourites with young Australians for many years.

Dorothy Wall's lively and amusing tales and delightful drawings make *The Complete Adventures of Blinky Bill* a book with immediate and lasting appeal for every child. this paperback edition, which includes most of the original illustrations, will be welcomed both by children who have already enjoyed Blinky's remarkable exploits and by those who have yet to make his acquaintance.

ISBN 0 207 16732 X

The Magic Pudding

By Norman Lindsay

The adventures of those splendid fellows Bunyip Bluegum, Bill Barnacle and Sam Sawnoff, the penguin bold, and of course their amazing, everlasting and very cantankerous Puddin'. A very unusual pudding it is indeed. Whistle three times, turn it round and it's steak-and-kidney if that's what you fancy, or hot jam roll, or delicious apple dumpling. Its manners are appalling, but it tastes so good! And it loves, just loves, to be eaten:

"Eat away, chew away,
munch and bolt and guzzle,
Never leave the table till you're
full up to the muzzle,"

it rudely urges the Noble Order of Puddin'-Owners, and of course the three members are delighted to oblige. But a secret like a magic pudding is hard to keep, and the envious eyes of professional puddin'-thieves are on the brave trio and their prize. The puddin'-thieves are cunning and masters of disguise, but no match in the end for the even greater ingenuity of righteous puddin'-owners.

ISBN 0 207 18864 5